WILD THING

WILD THING

Philip Norman

HEINEMANN : LONDON

William Heinemann Ltd
15 Queen St, Mayfair, London W1X 8BE
LONDON   MELBOURNE   TORONTO
JOHANNESBURG   AUCKLAND

First published 1972
© Philip Norman 1972
434 52302 X

Blues Next Door first appeared in *Playboy,* June 1972

Two lines from *The Sheikh of Araby* are reproduced by
permission of B. Feldman & Co. Ltd, 64, Dean Street,
London W1V 6AV.

Printed in Great Britain by
Northumberland Press Ltd Gateshead

For Lesley

Familia

Near Socorro, were those really cattle back there, shouldering down to a tunnel under the highway, trampling the desert edge with a noise of dry leaves? And cowboys and a chuck wagon which swivelled and jumped: cowboys perfect from a movie until the sun made a violent face of the wristwatch against a horse's neck. One may disbelieve one's eyes, but not the car radio. It said that firing on the White Sands missile range had been interrupted to allow the herd across.

In the green-shaded Cadillac, in the trailer equipped with an air-humidifier to protect the girls' voices, a spirit of westward movement is personified: the urge, not to travel but to get someplace. Day after day the horizon draws them to it. They may not rest until the sky itself does, in a dark wash behind traffic-signals overhead. The Ultimates open in Las Vegas less than forty-eight hours from now. Nothing must deflect this—not the cowboys Holly wanted to stop and see, nor the wrecks which curl occasionally through the dazzle of the facing lane; and never the drums, roadside boxes and gas-station Indians that were, one realized afterwards, a town.

Two quarter-pieces drop in the turnpike-trap. Real concentration is possible once more—road, land and sky open all into one white stare, flinching only with the thud of colour when another car passes. Then you are motionless again on boiling milk that streams back the way you came, then the trance breaks with the patter past of an ordinary Volkswagen, its driver kneeling up as if in prayer.

Somewhere, they went into Arizona. At Kingman, Ollive stopped on the truck terminal to phone the West Coast. But first he hesitated as a man does when about to be reminded, not that he's black but that he's dressed all in baby blue. Ollive put on shades which hid most of his face but not the sulky nostrils nor his belly; tender, sagging bequest of every supper-room where the Ultimates had played a midnight show. He told them to stay in the trailer.

Yet to stop was an event, even here. To be still, not wrapped by movement. To hear a definite construction-drill instead of that highway lullaby—hot winds, station-identification, signs whispering in the tail of the eye *Ain't you hungry yet?*—and to have the sun behind them. The sun was shut off by the body of a truck taller than any building Shirley and Holly had seen since St Louis; a truck with interstate licences that seemed to ascend to the sky, and a Navajo face on its cab, and silver and faintly trembling with refrigeration of the ten thousand TV dinners it carried.

Holly grabbed Shirley's arm and squeaked, 'There's a *lady* climbing into that!' Holly's curls were too many, her eyelashes like stars in charcoal by a child, but her mouth as she smiled shaped a perfect fish of white and dusty pink and the bright pink lateral line of her tongue. 'Damita Jo—come see here, Damita Jo!'

More than this was needed, however, to entice Damita Jo from the mouth of the humidifier while they were on the road. She was the last of the original

4

Ultimates of ten years ago. When Shirley, not herself, replaced Timmie Royale as lead singer, the fear seemed to intensify in Damita Jo that her voice must soon altogether disappear. Now, whenever she took the solo of even the simplest song, she tore into it as a puppy worries feathers.

'So a dumb girl's going three miles with a trucker and it gives him the right to a quick lay,' Damita Jo said unkindly from the coach, and cleared her throat.

'Ordinarily truckers don't give rides, Holly,' Shirley told her. 'Sometimes they have their wives go along to share the driving.'

Holly's spiky lashes stood awake at this.

'Shirley Hill, don't you know the darndest things! Where'd you get all of that education from?'

Damita Jo shouted, 'Bridget! Will you bring me a cup of tea, please.'

'Say—' Holly shone. 'Say, girls, wouldn't you just love to be a trucker's wife, huh, and sleep in back that way and share the driving?'

'Unreal,' Damita Jo said bitterly. 'You want a man so damned much, Holly why don't you marry that white boy, Earl?'

The white fish flew across Holly's mouth.

'Uh uh, not my type.'

'Well, I'll sure give him, he owns a heap of duplicator-machines.'

Damita Jo took the cup that Bridget their Nicaraguan maid had brought from the trailer kitchen. It was tea with the Cognac which soothed Damita Jo's throat and fears for her throat, and which already had carried her some way towards a lemon-peel and afternoon alcoholism in the interests of, as Damita Jo expressed it, 'cutting phlegm'.

'I'm going to go take a walk,' Shirley announced.

'—go take a *what*?'

'A walk out in the sun. Come with me, Holly.'

'Oh—but Ollive...'

'Ollive isn't through talking to Galahad.'

' "Yes sir" don't take so long,' said Damita Jo.

'Come, Holly.'

'Say listen, you two: how long you think Ollive's gonna stick around that terminal when he sees some trucker in the john with the door open?'

'Come, Holly. Maybe we'll find gourds.'

Her eyes fretted. 'Gourds?'

'Maybe arrowheads.'

'Just go right ahead, do anything you want,' Damita Jo said. She picked up a magazine and threw it down. After a decade of the same hit songs and cheeseburgers her attention rested upon nothing for long.

But Holly was nervous: of Damita Jo's sarcasm, of Ollive's tantrums, even of Shirley a little, though they liked one another in the slightly tongue-tied way of early real friendship. Shirley was by herself when she went out of the trailer, and really preferred this; out of the brocade and scented, faintly-damp interior into daylight that rang with heat like a shell.

The head of the truck began to move. Glowering, its silver case followed: its full face snarled at Shirley an instant; then, elegantly, endlessly, it all passed her. The sun was again set free.

The trucker's wife had the wheel. From on high, the trucker's wife wished she might have been so tall a black girl in a scarlet pants-suit hung with gold. Holly wanted somebody to love up to in the secret place behind the driving-cab—Shirley just imagined how it must feel *not* to be heading for Vegas and the lamps anchored on tables; the tasteless prawns. The trailer had crossed Oklahoma on a single freeway, after sudden cancellation of the Tulsa date. Shirley could remember what fresh

6

wind blew through the quarterlights in Oklahoma; and the forest in packed green cables running away below.

She drew level with another trailer, a fixture at the steel fence, with chickens walking round it. A white boy appeared through the screen door and stared at her. Shirley took off her glasses and for a moment was stunned by the shocking blue of the air.

'Are you hippies?' the boy inquired.

'Uh-uh.'

Such is the effect, in some places, of more bracelets than one.

'You goin' California?'

'No, to Las Vegas.'

'I want go California,' the boy told her. 'I want buy me a Jagwar and spend most days potting wheelies.'

'Excuse me?'

'Ain't you ever heard "potting wheelies" before?' The boy hoarsely described a method of driving, alleged to stand the Jaguar on its rear wheels like a stallion. 'My Dad,' he was saying, 'has a thirty-nine Ford XL Roadster and a three-window coup'; but now Shirley's attention was taken by the saddest of profiles. Motionless behind the steel fence, one bearded, venerable buffalo.

'You want to see the flush-toilet we have in back of our trailer?'

'Maybe I'll just take a stroll,' Shirley answered politely.

The boy stretched out a thin, pale arm without interest.

'There's hippies by the exit-road.'

He was encaged by the screen-door again; staring at her yet not daring to look, anxious for a friend but still turning away, his soul alert with a flashing dream of machines, his face already like a worried old man's. His shirt was patterned with his heroes. Shirley's heart moved for him.

7

Beyond the rough-bricked terminal gate on the other side of the road, two figures stood: a man and a child. Though at this distance they were merely cards outlined in heat, Shirley could tell that the man wore something tied round his head—that parts of his body were uncovered, perhaps even his feet—that he was exceptionable on the highway, where males are permitted only to display a bare forearm at the driving wheel.

She walked towards them—why? The urge not to travel but to get someplace. Another vehicle was leaving the terminal just then; a crumpled Oldsmobile of the same lizard-like antiquity as one in which Bridget the maid's Nicaraguan beau occasionally achieved a rendezvous with the trailer—the only beau who ever did. It paused at the gate before making a right into the system of support roads, curiously narrow and peaceful, that fed back into the highway's moving belt. It couldn't, even if it wanted, take the man and the child from the kerb, being already loaded far too close to the earth. It squeaked horribly and lagged away; departure of its tail fins revealing the child to be the man's wife. She held a baby. He stood, his arms chieftain-folded above her head.

Every nerve bred in by Hastings-on-the-Hudson, N.Y., clamoured against Shirley's approaching any nearer. Weren't the man in sandals and the girl, a pink dress to her bare feet—a threat, both of them, to the Sanitized world which bought albums by The Ultimates. She thought of Charles Manson and, in the heat haze, became chilled with fear. Then the girl's face looked up at her from the sleeping baby's. The girl then pushed hair behind her ear, the strand floating free again with the whirl of a truck on the highway below, and smiled with gums set far apart and small like a child's.

'Hi, there.'

8

'Hi, there,' Shirley answered, pitching it very light.

What came next, she knew, was 'Do you have any spare change?' but instead the man above lowered his head like a chieftain who descends to practicalities.

'Uh, you don't happen to want to buy an Indian hammock do you? It's known as a Familia because it can hold five persons. When the child grows, it builds one for itself.'

His eyes looked down at Shirley as if from the cool of a sunshade. The beard fitted his strong throat and teeth; he was taller than anyone in her life. With subtlety and neatness then, he spat into the roadside.

'She and I—' he nodded at the girl and baby, 'lived two years with the Indians on the—' and he spoke a name Shirley couldn't understand.

Declining the hammock, she said, 'Hitchin' a ride, huh?'

'That's correct. I'm Tarkin. This is my wife Penelope; my daughter Lulumae. If we had fifty dollars we could get us a car.'

'Where you headed for?'

'California.'

And Shirley looked up into the shade of his eyes and thought of California as people do everywhere—in Hastings-on-the-Hudson where oildrums guard the river; in Manhattan where they come out of their offices at noon to stare in the approximate direction of the sky—she saw pink blossoms through the shadow-bars of a venetian blind.

The Ultimates often played L.A., of course. Its air stung the skin. It was not always distinguishable from the filth haze round the elevator scrapyard at Yonkers.

'Come along with us,' Tarkin said.

'Whew—oh yeah!' Shirley attempted to recover as Penelope nodded agreement to this suggestion. 'Where at in California?'

9

'Big Sur, Hot Springs, California.

'Right next to the ocean,' Penelope said.

'A community lives there,' explained Tarkin. 'Understand: a while back the materialists all built large châteaux at Big Sur and then in the Recession, moved away. We stay there as caretakers. We make all of our own clothes and houses and instruments.'

His eyes left Shirley. Following them, she saw the emblazoned Police car resting sun-flattened on the brow of the overpass. In the octopus-eye on its roof, the sun glinted red.

'The Highway Patrol keeps an eye on us.' Tarkin's voice tightened almost imperceptibly. 'Just to see we don't forgo any of our privileges.'

'You sure are a long ways from home.'

His eyes returned to her.

'Once a year, a family is sent to buy vegetable products for the whole settlement. We eat no meat. In North California is where most vegetable products of the United States are manufactured. We made it part-business, part-vacation, but in Tepulpa our station wagon turned over in the main street.'

'All the products were in jars,' Penelope said. 'They rolled and popped on the road.'

'We retrieved maybe one per cent,' Tarkin added.

His eyes had wandered from Shirley again; she pursued them. Across its dry lake, the bright city of trucks gleamed. The patrol car had gone—but not far. There was nothing at all left on the crossroads above the highway: nothing, represented by a caterpillar. At the very gate of the terminal, in good order but exquisitely, with body-buckling care, it began to move outwards.

Softly, Tarkin remarked, 'When that caterpillar crossed that line, the Law of Karma came into effect.'

'Not if he's been a good caterpillar,' Penelope said.

They watched, not breathing. The baby, asleep. The

black moustache moved endlessly to the creamy middle of the road. When, long after that, it reached the safe dry grass, made itself an arch of thanks and vanished, Tarkin's eyes came back. He grinned jubilantly. And from the bundle on which she sat, Penelope turned to Shirley a face transfigured with happiness, as someone who finds a beautiful thing for you in a book.

'We rode a ways with a pipe-coverer,' Tarkin said presently. 'In a Mustang.'

'He treated oil-pipes with chemicals,' Penelope explained. She had been quietly singing to Lulumae. 'From Louisiana, and he sure did hate black folks. His life was all hate.'

'Enjoyable hate,' Tarkin said. 'Then we rode with a deputy-sheriff.'

'He wanted awful bad to shoot a person.'

Tarkin said, 'You know, Penelope, I thought that was his radio bag hanging on the suit-peg there. And two minutes later—it's a .38, he tells us, and he ain't about to hesitate to use it if he must.'

'Oh wow,' sighed Penelope.

'Then he asks, "You hippies aim to take over the Grand Canyon?" Then he says, "Know what I'd do with a man that won't get a job? I'd put him to work moving trees by hand." You understand what he meant? He meant forestation by hand.'

The noon violence had gone. The sun quavered small, like a hypnotist's light. There was a touch of blue china in the air, and the ability to look with eyes fully-opened exhilarated Shirley. She wanted to invite them back to the trailer—wanted to and yet was apprehensive, as one fondles a strange animal, half-fearing it will follow.

The point was settled by the arrival of Holly: Holly and curls and starfish eyes and white slippers, agitation but also delight at having found her, scandal because

Galahad at the West Coast said that she—Shirley—had
to cut out all the serious songs she'd been doing in the
show, and all the truckers came out of the terminal
restaurant to laugh at Ollive as he walked back, Holly
said, and Ollive was really mad and Shirley had to come
back right this—

Then Holly saw Lulumae.

Ollive's pink omelette mouth pouted.

'It's company policy. We're *nod* allowed to bring
guests into the trailer.'

'The baby's hungry.'

'I can't help that: we have to leave.'

Holly's eyes flashed—*Holly's*!

'We're getting milk for the baby, Ollive.'

They put Lulumae down on the brocade couch.
Damita Jo sprang up with an 'Oh my God!' From the
kitchen came Holly's voice and a tremendous opening
and shutting of the icebox door.

Penelope settled right away on the fawn rug, all her
bare toes lined up in the fluff; but not Tarkin. He
looked wrong, sitting. When Shirley spoke to him, he
merely answered her 'Yes, ma'am' 'No, ma'am' with an
hotel-boy emphasis. And his eyes now were not shaded.
They moved in frank bewilderment about the con-
fining draperies and silken magazines, while Ollive's
sulks filled the humidified air.

Presently Damita Jo came back into the living-room.
From her towel robe she had changed into white slacks
like Holly's; except that Holly's bore permanent creases
and Damita Jo's clung at the jug of her hips as flawless
as wax; and her shirt, of the lightest translucent yellow,
woke a buttercup reflection in the mink of her throat,
her unsupported, faintly shining breasts, and arms.

She sat on the couch beside Tarkin to regard him
with a face of insufferable beauty; as if the skin over
the cheekbones could scarcely contain the pointed green

eyes. In a mid-afternoon slur that had become habitual, she said to him, 'Reahlly—I'd love to know. I mean, when was it you took the *decision*—' Damita Jo chuckled a little helplessly. 'I mean, the clothes and—hair—and . . .'

Holly appeared, her glowing finger-ends spread against the baby's woollen back. She told them in a hushed voice, 'Lulumae drank her milk. Lulumae drank all of her milk.'

'I've been thinking a long time,' Damita Jo continued, 'that *I'd* like to do something different, you know? Like, follow some courses. Maybe in creative photography. You have any idea how I might start about that?'

'No, ma'am.'

'What sign were you born under?' she demanded.

Penelope had been sitting beside their feet. At times she would nod her chin to her knees, as a child will engross itself with private words while the grown-ups talk—now like a child that is captivated, she advanced in a straight line, fingers stretched out towards what she had seen.

The Ultimates' stage-wardrobe was divided from the living-room only by a curtain. At its parting, Bridget the maid appeared, stopped her with a gap-toothed smile, then yielded, and Penelope drew nearer.

She moved along the packed shoulders of the dresses, the compressed cascades. She touched the feathers, the powdery furs, the three gowns black-shot and heavy as armour, the three gowns that hung light and unreal like embroidered fire, all the gowns in threes. She gazed up at the bunched wet liquorice of the stage-wigs; the hats in threes and gold purses; the long gloves on their stands, clutching the air like trios of White House guests drowning formally behind a shelf.

In Holly's arms, Lulumae had moved. Penelope

13

turned, replacing the wisp of hair behind her ear, and again she and the baby became one thing.

'You really have to leave?'

'Yes we do.' Below the trailer step, his eyes looked up at her from shade once more. Inside, Holly's voice repeated, 'She drank her milk. Lulumae really drank her milk.'

Yet how, with time to wish a caterpillar across the road, could they be in any hurry?

Shirley began, 'Listen, I—'

'That pot scene?' Tarkin said mildly.

Damita Jo's final trick had been to produce from her luggage a parched, disintegrating but, to her, most wicked marijuana cigarette.

'Don't worry about it,' Tarkin said. Behind him, above the silver trucks, the sky detonated itself into purple. 'Lots of older folks like to show they real hip and on the weed. It amounts to the same as not knowing what to do with your hands.'

Above the baby's peaceful head, Penelope shut one eye against the sunset.

'Boy, is she unhappy deep down! And the one that held Lulumae and laughed—why can't she have what she wants?'

Tarkin gathered up the bundles he had left beside the step. Once again in a matter-of-fact voice he said, 'Come along with us.'

'By the ocean,' Penelope said, 'you do as you please.'

''Long as you don't infract on the rights of others,' Tarkin added.

'You all have drums next to the ocean?'

'Drums?'

Shirley was thinking of Hastings-on-the-Hudson.

A breeze stirred in Tarkin's eyes.

'We have ocean next to the ocean.'

14

As Shirley looked down to the cooling earth, all her confusion seemed to clear—Damita Jo as lead-singer—a new Ultimate out of High School into the thrill of her life—Holly could get along with anyone—and for an instant she could hear a boom of green milk and taste the wind that blows upon rocks. She answered:

'We open in Vegas tomorrow night.'

And the ocean vanished.

'Vegas—' Tarkin declaimed, hitching up his bundle. 'The air-conditioned city.' Penelope turned the baby to her other shoulder.

'We was in Vegas once,' she said. 'The folks all putting the dimes in 'fore they had a chance to pull the handles.'

'Remember the dead man we saw in Vegas, Penelope?'

'Dead? In an auto-wreck?'

'Nope,' Tarkin said. 'He was crossing the street. Had two bright ladies with him.'

Shirley remembered the patrol-car. 'Now you all take care yourselves and Lulumae—hear?'

'We'll be worrying about you,' Tarkin answered, 'inside your trailer.'

She was puzzled.

'We may not have your advantages,' Tarkin said, 'but you aren't free.'

This made her smile. 'Kids are the only free.'

'Not necessarily. Did you meet with a boy here on the terminal?'

'Sure. He was going to—'

'His Dad's two cars?' Tarkin said gently. 'They were mounted on blocks. They had no wheels to ride to California.'

'Hey!' Shirley protested; because she had nothing to give them, no pockets in her pants-suit, and then because she realized what it was that they had given her. It lay in her arms, strangely-moving, the most precious of all

15

their possessions. They were already far across the terminal: he striding, Penelope keeping up, her skirt raised a little from her ankles. And the detail was lost. They were man and child, and only a big and little finger to the spread, mauve fan of the sky.

Shirley held the Indian hammock for five persons.

A truck's new bright eyes hid them.

Wild Thing

In Northallerton, Yorkshire, Marvel and Jobete and Friends, featuring Reg Lubin, got up late as all tours do and attempted to breakfast in a chandeliered assembly-room already set for lunch. They were repulsed; not kindly. The hotel had been aggravated by the food-fight started by Lubin after the previous night's concert. Nor did conciliation advance in the behaviour of Marvel who, as a result of some later adventure in the northern streets, wore only a half of one leg of his jeans.

So they passed to a cocktail lounge which smelled of old cinema carpet but was proudly named *L'Aperitif*. That Marvel should be refused a cocktail here was no surprise. With his earring, his beard full of particles and his prickly, white leg, today more than ever he resembled Attila the Hun dressed for motor-bicycling. But when the barman was absent, Marvel returned. He leapt the quilted counter. Roaring, he began to mix for himself and his musicians certain unspeakable drinks.

The result was that, before the bus arrived to collect them, there were hours to wait outside on the pavement: unwashed, hungry, stung by the grime in the air, soaked by Reg Lubin's water-pistol, watched ferociously by a force of hotel porters and longingly by a small group of youths. One of them, as thin and white as Lubin, called out to him, 'You're great, Reg.'

On the bus, all sound withdrew into the mouth of the big road wind. His eye bumped the freezing glass at the back, always in the same place, and each time he awoke it was to some fresh illusion of arrival. There was the death-roar of passage across a suspension-bridge. A slag-heap drifted by, stuck with clean pins like a city of night clubs.

The tour had lasted all of Robb's life. In The Friends he played rhythm-guitar; at the back of the stage as of the bus. There is little snobbery among Rock musicians, since anyone is a genius who says he is. Even the presence of one of the authentic half-dozen genii had excluded Robb from none of the larks—a food-fight, the sharing of drugs through a carved pipe. It was by temperament that he occupied places where light did not fall.

Robb wished for it to continue, just as people grow timorous at leaving hospital, yet even he could see the end of the tour closing rapidly. Darlington was left to play, and Newcastle-upon-Tyne. Then they were booked for a week of one-nights in Scandinavia and for recording-dates after that. Against the whim of superstars, however, such obligations are less than nothing.

Reg Lubin had decided it would be fun to go back on the road again. Why Lubin should believe so was mysterious to Robb, but for as long as the fun could last, he sheltered in it and tried to snatch sleep in the dusty warm of the bus-heater, the dubious welcome of the northern hotels. All of it was subsidised by Lubin; every half-empty Civic hall. Nor had any expense been spared to make the attending detail, the rubbish of ice-cream paper, crusts and lager bottles, exactly as Lubin remembered it.

This had continued three days already, but Lubin's

pleasure in this novelty—squalor—showed no sign of abating. At the front of the bus, a constant giggle of springs came from his seat. That afternoon in the queue of a motorway café he had turned to Robb, grinning, and asked to borrow a pound to buy a cup of tea. And he'd paid for the equipment too, airfreighted from Los Angeles; and in each draughty changing-room they occupied, his five guitars winked from caskets lined with silks of red and burnt orange.

Even Robb, at the back, could hardly remember concerts so bad as these. None so far had been better than a rehearsal; but fortunately, paying Rock audiences are accustomed to witnessing rehearsals. Last night in Northallerton they had arrived onstage an hour late. By the time the obligatory twenty minutes more had been taken up by the band—to test microphones already tested, to tune-up and show what wild little personal riffs each of them knew—the waiting darkness was filled with screams. Not for the band nor for Marvel nor Jobete: for Lubin to play on his own.

But Marvel believed it was all for him. In the intervals of drinking from a beercan, the whelk of his bearded lips assumed a regal expression. He started to behave like a star. Unluckily for the audience this, in Marvel's estimation, did not include the playing of music. Pausing at times to refresh himself from the beercan, as the screams increased he began to talk to them through the public-address system. *'Get on with it, Reg!'* the desperate voices begged; and Marvel, overwhelmed by the grandeur of this welcome, shook his black ringlets and, beatifically, talked to them.

The voices wailed, *'Reg.'*

They sent up entreaties of love: grown men with but a simple dream to change places with Lubin. Flourishing the beercan, Marvel embraced them all and Lubin, behind him, merely grinned. The tour must last as long as his infatuation did with Marvel; as long as it amused Lubin to smash milk-bottles with Marvel and break wind as fearlessly as Marvel did. He had even started to grow a beard like Marvel's. He himself was so thin that onstage sometimes all you could see were his sleeves.

All the lights had been turned up in the Corn Exchange, revealing the shadow and wonder of the stage as only a mess of cables. Under the skyline of silent equipment Robb knelt—not investigating the shrieks of feedback which had, likewise, destroyed the Darlington concert; just kneeling there. A few last raincoats cleared disappointedly through the furthermost exists.

Finally he got his knees to rise and went back to the changing-room, which stood in the region of the boilers. Lubin and Marvel had left, and almost everyone else. There is, as already stated, little snobbery among Rock musicians; but a superstar and his favourites have power to remain invisible for long periods. A lot of orange peel was left behind, a black man in an embroidered sheet softly played a talking-drum, and another unemployed guitarist; a displaced person from the band that had been destroyed by Lubin when he began to worship Marvel and Jobete. To the smiling black man, the guitarist was trying to explain how it felt to be out of work. 'I just have to get myself together,' he said tragically. The black man smiled. Robb discovered that six pounds had been stolen from his jacket.

There were girls, of course, outside every stage-door; girls of fourteen and fifteen with black stares and bloodless lips, but they weren't for such as Robb. They did not acknowledge the back of the stage. They waited to be pressed one at each side of a superstar's furs, with their ancient eyes staring out, like cats being carried. Therefore Robb hardly saw the two who came up to him outside the Corn Exchange, and hardly looked, since

22

both of them wore long coats and woollen bonnets rather as children bundled up for play. He automatically mentioned going back to the hotel for a drink. He didn't want them. He wanted to take off his boots.

'A drink, what of?'

'I'm not,' the other girl declared. 'I'm goin' for to catch th'eleven-ten bus.'

'And I'm not goin' without *her*.'

His head turned away from the wind, Robb was aware of a transaction.

'Ee, go on, man, have a drink with him. You *are* a group, aren't you?' the first girl demanded.

'That one was with Reggie Lubin; I seen his hat, Vivien.'

'Then away and have a drink with him. I'll catch me eleven-ten bus.'

So Robb went along the colonnade to the main street with his face turned inwards, and one of the girls kept up with him in a series of little impacts by her toe against her long coat. On the final pillar, in letters five feet high, someone had spray-painted LUBIN IS GOD. They came out into the light. Instead of disappearing, the girl grabbed his arm.

'Ee!' she exclaimed. 'I was just sayin' to Vivien that's caught th'eleven-ten bus, would it not be awful if Reggie Lubin got hisself kidnapped!'

Her lips, parted with the horror of the idea, revealed two little serious rabbit's teeth—the yellow light painted the cheeks inside her bonnet as brilliantly as jam.

'Well, whereabouts do you live?' he asked helplessly.

'W'call 'em the Dwellings. They're prefabs. Do you say "prefabs" down in London, Robbie?'

The use of his name startled him.

'They're dinky,' she said. Her face shone with affection. 'No room in 'em for to store a suitcase or anything of that sort.'

'I'll put you in a taxi then, all right?'

'No,' she said, 'I'll stick with you.'

The hotel doors were locked. They came, walking beneath the gargoyles of majestic northern banks, to the blue mouth of a club where he knew some of the band would be. She recoiled in horror, saying, 'Ee, *no*, I canna' go in there; don't ask us.'

'Why not?'

'Ee, I *can't*. That Greek chappie got thrown downstairs, and broke his collarbone and bit his tongue. Don't ask us, Robbie.'

She shivered. Each time she said 'no', it was pert refusal as well as sighing reproof. She had walked on a little farther with her nose in the air, and now stood against a darkened shop, holding her coat shut with both hands. Robb did not hesitate; he simply was of a type that loiters indefinitely before a light. Then he felt her eye on him. And it fell to the rhythm guitarist from the back of the stage—and occasionally the back of the van on a pile of amplifier-tarpaulins—to provide the decent alternative.

She had pointed out items of interest such as the Darlington town clock, the high-level shops and Covered Market. Now, under dead trapezes of the trolley-bus system, they walked along an endless high road. The town lay below the hedge: lights thinly dispersed around the elephant feet of two identical gasometers.

Once she turned and faced him, flushed by another lamp-post, and softly exclaimed, 'Ee, you booger, you're not talkative, are you?'

'No.'

'Then I'll go.' But this was merely a rebuke, a further inflection of her voice that Robb did not understand. He had been walking only dimly aware of a presence on a lower level than himself, conversing busily, and the little dull thuds at the skirts of her coat. Were his

24

trousers real leather? Did he get his money in a pay-packet, like, once a week? Did he have to pass examinations in 'electrics'? He was a top pal of Reggie Lubin's, though, wasn't he?

'Don't lie,' she said. 'Y'have it all easy, don't you?'

'I don't think so, no.'

'Ee, of course you do! Secretaries waitin' on you, I bet.'

He laughed ironically.

'Robbie, why do you walk with your head on one side. Is it because of your hair blowin' back?'

'Look, I don't know,' he answered savagely.

'Don't you curse me, just because your hair's goin' back.' She primly hit his arm. 'Ee, man, there's not much gristle on you!'

'Just don't keep watching me, okay?'

'You don't like bein' watched, do you?'

'No.'

'There's the Beck over there,' she said. 'It's not very hygienic, I'm afraid.'

The wind cried and waved the hedge with the town beyond it. Marvel and Reg Lubin were in the town somewhere throwing a cold buffet at one another. Robb had no imagination: none. But sometimes he shut his eyes, opened them and wondered how he'd got here.

'This is me aunty's house, with the rose-arch. Are you comin' in, Robbie?'

She threw up her arms. In the shadow, her chin disappeared, her neck was pulled like a goose, her hair stood on end and finally she emerged from the woollen bonnet, and smiled down at him.

'They're a job to get off, them helmets, but th'keep a head very warm. Are you comin' in?'

'"Coming in?"'

'Just me Uncle Valentine's at home,' she said.

Her uncle came from the kitchen. He was not an old

25

man, but toothless. He wore a stiff collar and black uniform tie. Under a bright light he questioned Robb as to the life and expectations of a rhythm-guitarist in order to allow himself to say, 'Ah'm musical too, y'knoa and all that. Oh ay.'

'I'll take Robbie in The Room for ten minutes, Uncle Valentine,' she told him.

'Ay all right—*and* I've got castanets here too,' her uncle said, 'I danced with a Spanish lass and all once, down Shields way. And it weren't in a dance-hall mind, it was in our own house.'

'Me little brother Dave'll probably be in and out,' she said. She pressed the door closed with her shoulder as, from the other side, her uncle's voice continued, '—and I've known the Mighty y'knoa, back and forth on the boats—'

Her hair was cut in the lampshade of a million other girls. She wore her cardigan back-to-front. She laughed: 'He's only little, me Uncle Valentine, but he's joyful.'

She sat down beside the electric fire with its belly of artificial coals, tugging her skirt around the edge of her knees.

'Robbie: do you still get many of them four-letter words down in London?'

He was at the window, trying to shelter from the terrible overhead light. Among the curtains, his hand displaced a Spanish doll shut in a cylinder. The curtains were of plastic. Outside, in lighted bands, a bus ground up the hill.

'Me mam and me don't get on together all that well,' she was explaining. 'W'have words, Robbie, that's what w'do, and I live at me Uncle Valentine's at the moment. A lot of the time it's due to her constantly goin' on about Mario Lanza.'

'Yeah,' he said, looking out.

'But she generally comes around, later on. She'll say

26

to us "Do you fancy a meat sandwich for your tea?" '

Turning from the curtains, Robb almost knocked her face.

'Look, I said don't watch me!'

'I can't help seein' you—you look desperate, man,' she told him.

The door was hurled open. A boy entered, breathing heavily, and disappeared from sight behind the armchair. Without acknowledging their presence he began to search for something. His nose was very blocked.

'Dave's doing some printing,' she remarked.

The boy responded by the zoom of a friction-toy.

'Dave: for your birthday do you want a party or a big present?'

'A big present,' the boy answered.

She suddenly put both arms around Robb. He looked down at this as if from a great height. There was a Grenadier on the window-sill, also shut in a corsage-box. Her hair smelled of the electric-fire.

'Robbie,' she sighed, 'you're freezin' cold.'

He stumbled.

'Eh, watch w'don't topple over, man,' she warned riotously. Her face was tipped up against the stale leather of his chest. At the rim of her cheeks she had drawn little irregular eyelashes.

'Me boss brought me the Spanish doll. I've not been abroad; only to Holland for the day,' she said, and squeezed him again. Behind the chair the boy arose, still breathing massively. 'Dave,' she called.

'Yes, Jeanette.'

'Out the light for us, man, will you?'

The boy did so. She guided Robb carefully over as if he was blind and sat him down. Newspapers rasped under the cushions of the chair.

'I think it was Amsterdam where we were—we saw the fields of flowers all round us.'

27

'Ooh.' His shoulders collapsed in the ashes of exhaustion.

'It was canny,' she continued. 'Me aunty put me name down with the school-cleaners, unofficial—hey, you canna' put 'em straight near the fire! Ee, Robbie! How do you ever play the 'lectric guitar with hands like them?'

'One request.' His eyes were closed. 'Don't crack me fingers around too much.'

She held them coldly and clearly between her own, kneeling up between his legs. 'Ee, Robbie,' she sighed, 'the joints are like winter.'

The door flew open, the light went on. She remained between his knees; all he could feel was the fire against the shins his boots had entombed. The coals drew him, staring, among their lightweight crags. Dave, with a nose still very blocked, inquired over their heads, 'Me Uncle Valentine says do you fancy a biscuit and cheese?'

'Was that not gentle enough, Robbie?'

He had sat up in agony. Between his belt and his shirt, his ribs showed like a greyhound. He relaxed again. The newspapers creased underneath him.

'What are those on the wall then? Wings?'

'They were off me Uncle Valentine's goldfinch,' she said. 'He couldna' bear to bury all of it. Did I hurt you, Robbie—pullin'?'

'It's all right. I've got a bad back.'

'A disc,' she said wisely. 'Me boss had one of them and they racked her for it. She said it was not much fun.'

'Yeah, it's really terrible, just like two strings snapping. You know—down your leg.'

'But Robbie. How did you get a disc from playin' the 'lectric guitar?'

'Well, I think it must have been a bit on the heavy side for me.'

'Shall I tell you where the warmest place is?'

But he watched the fire. The fire swam red through

the branches of his eyes. Her face was only an almond in the fire.

'In between me clothes,' she said. 'If you want, Robbie, you can put your hands in between me clothes.'

According to the booking-agent, the Beatles had played Newcastle City Hall on their very last tour. Commemorating this, a mounted constable stood over the silent queue that waited with hands up its sleeves on both sides of varnished doors which the auditorium shared with the Public Baths.

Behind the stage, Marvel and Jobete and Friends stared resentfully at the accommodation provided for them by the Newcastle city fathers. It was neither changing-room with duck-boards nor ante-room to a boiler-house, but a Blue Room furnished with sofas of chintz.

Then doors were folded open from the corridor. A horse artillery of civic waitresses sped in; pert and scrubbed little women with silver hair and blue hair and smiles intimating 'you bad boys', and trays of metal coffee pots and hot-water jugs. As they laid the long table, they also efficiently collected the autograph of everyone in the room, even Robb. 'Will you do it for Sharon—and June—and for little Willis?' An astonished hole opened in Marvel's beard and he was whirled to one side by the unbillowing of a tablecloth. 'Mind yourself, pet,' a tiny creature commanded.

Reg Lubin had not yet arrived. This was the first day of the tour he had not entirely spent in Marvel's company; whooping, hugging, leg-wrestling; and so, in the later afternoon in Newcastle, Marvel had been thrown on his own devices. All he could think of to do, apart from beating up Jobete, was to linger on the pavement outside a Co-operative supermarket. As respectable women came out, Marvel followed them with his one bare leg. He pranced on his toes an instant behind them.

29

He bellowed against their hat-pins, 'Wheee-hoo-*eee*, will ya look at that *butt!*'

When Lubin finally did appear in the Blue Room, a ferocious-eyed girl pressed one at each side of his furs, he seemed no different. He had shaved off the beginnings of his beard—the beard like Marvel's—but his absence from Marvel that afternoon bore no sinister explanation; Lubin, as usual, had simply rushed off to find a joke-shop, but without Marvel. What he had bought this time for a laugh were some horrible little clockwork fruit: lemons and oranges and a scarlet pear, which had legs and faces, and walked and dragged their feet.

Lubin set them all off among the refreshments. At this, the eyes of Marvel brightened like two cigarettes inhaled at once. He allowed Jobete to rise from the tray of fancy cakes into which he had been grinding her face. He and some of the band started to hold races with the fruit, Marvel himself favouring the pear.

Marvel shrieked, 'Go, Big Red—c'mon, Red—go, go go, Red!' He laid his beard along the tablecloth, and beside him Jobete sat knitting. She wore yellow snake boots and small pebble-glasses. With a black girl from the backing-group, she harmonized 'Oh Happy Day'; and like smoke, like a beatitude, the words drifted across a Blue Room already affected by spat-out bread and care-less boot-heels. Lubin's fur coat lay over a chair. Robb sat within the chair and the coat. The red pear walked unsteadily among the coffee-pots. Lubin had lost interest in the races and disappeared again. The pear struck the edge of a sugar-basin and toppled back. It grinned, Marvel implored it to rise. Its legs waved feebly.

The walls of the Blue Room were papered with two distinct motifs, civic seahorses and municipal swallows. They were divided exactly at eye-level by the glass frieze of an older, more beautiful decoration, and the whole door leading out to the Gents' was a mirror. This now opened, throwing aside the reflection of Marvel. Reg Lubin reappeared with his hair soaking wet.

Against the frieze he stood and used a comb. He patted and shaped the slappy mass above his forehead, smoothing it through the joins of his ears. Then he crammed it behind his neck into the kind of foliation that the ravers wore twenty years ago; that Lubin himself, being only nineteen, might never have seen at all, but for the passage of the tour-bus through some Durham pit-village or other. Then he turned round.

The face was Lubin's; yet nobody ever quite remembered the face; only the touch of illness against its pointed eyes. Its shape had changed completely with the curving of the hair above like the front of a swing-boat. True, the boots were still Lubin's, and the expensively-aged clothes of one colour, and the grin. That unemployed guitarist, if no one else, should recognize the grin, for it had presaged the destruction of his own, and many previous, splendid bands. The grin signified precisely the moment at which the superstar's attention, mind, body and soul were attracted by some fresh novelty.

'*Hey!*' The others took it up. All did but Marvel who, in his concern for Big Red, did not perceive in Lubin's new hair-style the end of his and Jobete's European tour. All but Robb as well, to whom survival on the road meant conservation of all movement. But to the lump of Rock bands, survival, as well as music, reposes in faithful copying. They laid down saxes and cress-sandwiches and everyone ran and wet his hair.

To go with the hair, they did nothing that night but old things like *Rip It Up*, with cowlicks and quiffs shaking over their faces; and, since these songs demand real work and eliminate all pretence, the last concert of the tour was wonderful. Marvel and Jobete, sharing the microphone, sang with a pure one-note, like the

31

sound of an instrument, as if they were really in love. As Lubin's sleeves moved out to join them in the light, a delighted lunatic pranced up the aisle, the lunatic was restrained and the applause spread out to form a flickering continent in the darkness.

...At the back of the stage it is not so bad. In that pocket of quiet far behind the storming loudspeaker faces, the senses grow keen among the electric dust. Equipment consoles make the noise of larks. A road manager coughs. There is a smell from the amplifier fabric like warm luggage. The eyes rest outwards in a cup of purple twinkling with green Exit signs...

Then that lunatic came back. He jumped up to join them. Hands from below culled him back into his proper obscurity. He jumped up on the stage once more— and prevailed. He danced, bending forward, his hair toppling forward, as if he carried his house on his back. His hair was combed into a swingboat like theirs; but it was in earnest. He wore a coat to his knees and trousers which gripped his ankles, and socks of tangerine.

Another one followed him, and another. The stage became filled, the band totally hidden, by juddering cylinders of cloth upon the backs of worshippers preserved from the past, who swooped and bopped and performed feats of bending backwards which seemed almost to cut their long coats in two. On the tiers behind, on either side of the pipes of the city organ, lines of them stiffly gambolled like figures on a German clock: they bopped even on the balconies. They hid everyone— everything but the sound to which, in homage, they bopped. You could not even see Lubin's sleeves. But from within the joyous thud of cloth came the voice of a guitar; a voice, since its very action seemed changed. It was more than wood and wire, shaped through the blow of a thousand watts, it was molten metal blended with metal cool and sharp like fresh tin.

A Street of City Lights

In the low, thin Cadillac he sat up like a baby in its chair. His collar shone and the rings of his cuffs as they turned the wheel at the farthest diameter of his arms. Not to his apartment, where Winston S. Churchill's *History of the English-Speaking Peoples* awaited, but to the city; down to lines of yellow and blue beads that slid over the cushion of night.

The miracle of Oscar Taliaferro among fizzling cicadas was that he was here. Skouras and Ventura and Demetriou had gone, each lightly broiling Oscar all over in the fires of their collapse. His clothes were perfect, since he could no longer make any movement to disturb them, and one eye was shut. The other gleamed like glass.

Since the Unpleasantness, by which Oscar meant his stroke, a little publicity was all he handled. Publicity at Buzzy Bee International and at cocktail hour, out of regard for Buzzy, he kept the beers coming from the icebox. A lot of people, mostly song-pushers, dropped by the office around six-thirty. Buzzy himself sat at the bar; a seated pear. Behind the counter, Oscar told the visitors they were in the presence of a remarkable, re-markable man and Buzzy, save for the enormousness of his breathing, remained modestly silent.

'In three years, the biggest Country music talent agency on Harmony Row,' Oscar's dry bark proceeded. 'You know how many millionaires they already had in this place? Eight hundred.'

But when Oscar bent to the ice-tray with a squeak of the irons on his legs, sometimes Buzzy grasped the shoulder of the person next to him and exclaimed:

'*Tha'* guy!'

And the violet mounds of Buzzy Bee's eyes would fill with a tender amazement.

'Tha' guy painted sparrows to resemble canaries. In the olden days. Tha' guy is fantastic!'

He rested in the afternoons in Buzzy's own suite. But the leg still pained him tonight from a thousand wires; his stomach felt curdled by another of Buzzy's lunches. Of the twittering dark, all that Oscar Taliaferro desired was the prose of W. S. Churchill, then, without remedial harness, to sink to the centre of the earth. First he had to drive to an all-night Drug on Blue Grass Boulevard because he was out of Ovaltine.

Blue Grass was the strip. It pooled its illuminations in the sides of tour-buses and the contact-lenses of those within, searching for a Country music hero along the sidewalk. But the tourists, and all the kids who flocked here with guitars on their backs, would profit from consulting a street-map first. A map showed the Strip's contiguousness, in the matter of dreams, to absolutely nothing. Harmony Row—the record-companies, the offices of Buzzy Bee International—all stood eight blocks higher towards the stars.

Against Oscar's collar, lights marched like yellow bees, turned in red, flung sails and, in mauve and pink wheels, spread out, withdrew and spread out. From on high, the huge, chucky countenances of cowboy kings smiled down on him and on their own quick roast-beef franchises. The cowboy kings themselves were in Florida or politics, or concealed in curious-smelling, ranch-style bungalows. The Strip ran for ninety yards. Then the used-car lots continued, out of the valley to the end of the world.

The all-night Drug had disappeared. In its place was the P. Cox Mountain Lair. A play on words this, since the bar contributed to wonderland a bird with a three-colour gushing tail under which a man in grey drill stood listlessly reading a newspaper.

Past the man Oscar saw an empty green barn whose discreet jukebox had no connection with the scrawl of wild Country violins released to the street. A hag in white boots danced with the solitary customer, pumping his arm conscientiously. 'I'll dance with you,' she reproved the customer, 'but I won't sleep with you.'

'That's awful,' Oscar said. But he had to rest.

He had almost summoned breath enough to return to the car when a kid got up beside the pinball machine and sang and played guitar like Seldon Redman back from the dead; and the rill of discovery leapt through Oscar Taliaferro, independent of harness and medicament, from days long ago. And no one else was around to grab it.

So what? Every kid that came in on the bus expected to make a million dollars by copying Seldon. Buzzy Bee already had Seldon Junior under contract; if that wasn't trouble enough. And *he* wasn't paid to find new acts for Buzzy, only to handle a little publicity now and again, as the doctor ordered.

Oscar went over and spoke to the kid. He was doing this, he told himself, purely for Buzzy. After the Unpleasantness, it was Buzzy who had been first to offer him a way back. The silver lady's leg with which, at cocktail-hour, he opened the soft-drinks, represented yet another

37

gift of kindness he had received of Buzzy Bee. After some moments with the kid, however, Oscar viewed this debt as having substantially been repaid.

The kid, Charles Pinkard from Arkansas, was a dumb young creep. Impossible that he had ever resembled the genius Seldon Redman or that the voice which now mumbled 'Yes, sir,' 'No sir,' had drawn, like Seldon's, all tragedies from life from the yodel of babyhood to the bass of desperate age, or that the stained fingers smacking a cigarette to the kid's lips had pulled such notes in *Mule-Skinner Blues*. He grinned at empty smoke. It did not surprise Oscar to hear that Charles Pinkard had been playing along the Strip for eight weeks in various bars and now, the end of the tourist-season, still earned only what his girl could collect around the booths in a cigar-box.

'She your wife?' Oscar demanded. 'Or sweetheart?'

As she gurgled at this, hiding in the oily ropes of the kid's neck, Oscar imagined he had seen the girl before somewhere. But she was a child. The cigarette was large between her fingers. A child's pointed face; the button ears of a child from which arose a tall, intricately-curled and cabled yellow pompadour. 'Charles,' she echoed. 'Oh—*Charles*!' She wore a shirt that matched his, and covered him continually with kisses.

A hand wearing an identity-bracelet, curved towards Oscar from the third person in the booth.

'Rock Rivers's my name. From Texas.'

Oscar ignored the hand.

'Good evening.'

'Glad to see you,' Rock Rivers said.

He was older than the other two and, by the self-possessed and wise manner in which he leaned on the archway of his cuffs, revealed to Oscar at once that he was living off them. He spoke in a rich, deep voice as if providing the sound commentary to some religious spectacle. From his peak of hair, occasionally a long piece detached itself and hung beside his face.

'And you're a singer also?'

'Anywhere I can,' Rock Rivers answered tranquilly, replacing the piece of hair.

Oscar's eye, being most exquisitely tuned to detection of every sort of bum, would have left Rock Rivers then. But the girl, nipping Charles Pinkard's ear, sucking him under the chin, finally pulled his whole head down to her: their mouths, to Oscar's horror, joined like the struggling halves of a clam.

'And you, too, intend to be a big star?'

'Did you ever meet anyone that had designed their dream-house?' Rock Rivers inquired sonorously.

Oscar snapped, 'I didn't get you.'

'I designed my own dream home.'

'For when you achieve stardom.' Oscar looked at him.

'Plans are all drawn up.' With sudden energy Rock Rivers took out a pocket-book of failure, bulging with out-of-date cards. His face, as he turned the paper round to Oscar, was transformed; his snub cheeks assumed that expression of ingenious wonder with which a dolphin beckons from an aquarium poster,

'You think that's a flying-saucer. They're houses built for people at the Lake; aluminium. I plan,' Rock Rivers said, 'to have twenty-four of 'em, all connected by passages. Here, the steps come out of the house. You watch on close-circuit TV here.'

'For the fans, uh?'

'Right.' The hair fell and hung beside Rock Rivers' face again. ''F you wanna see 'em, fine. If not, tell 'em to go away. But I'll always see 'em.'

'Because they love you,' Oscar said.

'Your most precious possession.' The claw of hair was replaced. 'And in back here, I'll put in a garden. I'll put in okra—Chinese chestnuts, paper-shell pecans. Here—'

39

he rested his chin on his wrists, 'here I'll have a perfect replica of Le Mans. The racing-circuit. That's for me to play in.'

'A star needs a wardrobe,' Oscar said.

'My clothes—I'll have all in two colours. Gold. And grey.' His voice was resonant now, as if Rock Rivers spoke the words of a ballad. 'Grey was Seldon's favourite colour.'

'You intend to be a big star like Seldon Redman.'

'Someday,' Rock Rivers answered quietly.

'But how old are you, fink?' Oscar said.

'Huh?' His calm mouth fell at the corners—all the quiet and wisdom gone. His face was grey. He was terrified.

'Charles,' Oscar said, turning back, 'I want you to come by my office. If you have a tape, bring one. Did you ever cut your own session? How do you spend the day—*what*?' he demanded. He was very nearly exhausted.

The kid swallowed. 'Just—goof around, 'spose.'

'You ever go to college, Charles?'

Into the girl's shining face he answered, 'No sir, guess not.'

'That's awful,' Oscar said.

'Sir?'

Oscar leaned forward on the head of his stick.

'You know how to retain a good constitution, Charles; know what you ought to do? Learn one new fact every day.'

The kid looked directly at him for the first time.

'About any topic whatever,' Oscar said, 'about world coinage or some interesting new species. Charles, if you listen or you don't listen, I'll tell you this, it is impossible to overestimate the value of education.'

The girl said, 'Charles tells me 'bout those Romans sometimes.' He looked down at her.

40

'Yeah, we had pretty good talk this afternoon 'bout the Romans.'

'The Aediles,' she said. 'M'hm, and the Lictors and that ol' Mucius when he done thrust his hand in the furnace.'

'Myself, I am reading *History of the English-Speaking Peoples* by Winston S. Churchill.'

She sighed. 'Man, that's heavy. That 'bout those Romans?'

'It expands the mind,' Oscar said. 'Charles, you wanna be a big star of Country and Western. You play a goodeal of Seldon Redman material—'

'Like Jerry Lee, too, don't you, hon?' she said.

'—pulling the notes that Seldon pulled is not enough. Seldon expanded his mind.'

Fans of smoke were suddenly expelled from the nostrils of Charles Pinkard.

'You *knew* Seldon?'

'I knew him certainly.'

'Hot damn,' said Charles Pinkard.

Her eyes shone in half-moons. 'Wow, say, would you tell us about him?'

'How'd he ever sing like that?' Charles Pinkard asked weakly.

'It was a matter of his wanting to accomplish a great deal of it,' Oscar replied, 'for his mother.'

'Oh wow, he was sure great!'

'He tried so hard to be great that finally he was,' Oscar said. 'I was with Seldon the night he passed away.'

'Hot damn,' Charles Pinkard said. The girl tittered: 'They sure kept on passing away, these good ol' ...'

Oscar prepared to speak. The girl and Charles Pinkard both looked at him.

'—You mentioned health. I still have to insure my hands,' said Rock Rivers.

41

'I didn't get you,' Oscar snapped.

'I still have to insure my hands. As deadly weapons.'

With a cigarette in his mouth Rock Rivers picked up a beercan and, with the air of a great illusionist, flexed his hands around it. As the girl's attention dropped from Oscar, once again he felt he had seen her before somewhere. But she was just a child, giggling. Rock Rivers' pocket book still lay on the table of the booth like a beached whale. She foraged lovingly through the folds of Charles Pinkard's premature belly and picked out a snapshot.

'Wow! Rock, you wore a beard!'

'Used to,' he admitted modestly.

'Is that the wife you lived with in the trailer?'

'Nope.' The cigarette jumped as he prepared for his feat of strength. 'Just a chick I was foolin' round with.'

Oscar said, 'You mean you have a *wife*?'

'Oh yeah,' he said, concentrating.

'He has two little boys,' the girl bleakly added.

Rock Rivers shrugged.

'They understand,' he said with quiet wisdom.

Ash bending from his cigarette, with eyes closed and one deadly hand he squeezed the beercan. He intensified the pressure. He brought the other hand up to it. His shoulders grew tense and the finger of hair dropped beside his face as, with two hands, he fought to crush the beercan.

Oscar took it away.

'What do they "understand"?' he said. 'Tell us what they "understand", fink.'

Oscar set down the beercan. He had strangled it like an hourglass. On the balcony of his lip, a little moisture shone.

Buzzy's vice-president Merle Schaeffer was still in

Europe. Buzzy himself, in a chocolate ruffle shirt swaggering over the tyres of his neck, had to present a colour TV at a children's hospital. And so would Oscar talk— just talk—to Seldon Redman Junior, who was in town?

'Very well,' Oscar said.

Buzzy put an arm round him. He was the one person in the world who could do so.

'I 'prishiate it—so much.'

'But his Mamma wants my ass,' Oscar added.

Buzzy gazed stertorously after him as he left the room, and to the receptionist whispered, 'Could you believe tha' guy, Miss Bronsen? Tha' guy was the first to make one million dollars in Country and Western. In the olden days. And you know how much he lost? A million and a half.'

Charles Pinkard did not come by the office as agreed, which was a blessing. Oscar's day had been sufficiently disturbed. He had dreamed last night, for the first time in twenty years, and, being deeply superstitious, had awoken thinking it to be a portent of his death. That morning he had fallen, although not seriously, in the bathroom. Now: the heir to the genius of Seldon Redman.

In white, purple-frogged satin, the heir lay like a silkworm, all immobile purple fringes, in Buzzy's Chinese Room, his cowboy boots on the bamboo coffee-table, scattering and snapping peanuts from the ornamental candy-jar. His bottom-lip, irrespective of any surprise, hung out as if to dry. He did not get up if an older person entered the room.

Junior listened and spat and Oscar, for the fourth time, began, 'Here is the box-number of a corporation. A mail-order corporation out of Newark, New Jersey—'

Junior had as yet enjoyed no marked success in the Country Music charts, even though five or six of his late father's albums still coasted in and out; and shameless attempts were continually made by studio-engineers to transform the kid's fat voice into that same elvish magic.

He seemed nevertheless, to have dulled Buzzy's normal acuteness. His visits to Buzzy Bee International were accorded the privileges of a maharajah. His publicity, in fact, was under the personal supervision of his mother; most of it depicting him down on one knee, a chiffon scarf tied below his ear, cracking a bullwhip. Buzzy, however, made supplementary gestures; such as circulating to important people in the music industry, gold keys inscribed 'From the homestead of Seldon Redman Junior'. It was this plan that Oscar had been asked to elucidate.

'Your recipient,' he explained, 'has only to send his gold key to the box-number in Newark, together with his own ignition-key—'

'S'posin' he don' got no automobile?' the heir to the Redman genius inquired.

'—or his apartment key. He can send the key to his apartment.'

... Echoes of his own voice, Oscar had dreamed; his voice when there was still moisture in it, ringing across a ballroom in Rockaway, Long Island. And the Genuine Twelve-Inch Hot-dog racket. The Indian who bent a seven penny weight railroad spike. The two ladies who took him upstairs in West Palm Beach, saying they wanted to show him something; and he thought it was a work of art they wanted to show him, something like that...

'The gold key is returned,' Oscar continued, 'subsequently cut the same way as the ignition-key. Or the key to the apartment.'

Mrs Myra 'Mickie' Seldon Redman, the custodian of genius, wore a lemon coat with hanging sleeves in the style of the Queen of England. Her hair, though elaborately pinked and coiffed, was suspended a little apart from her well-powdered head—and something about that hair put Oscar in mind of Rockaway again, the ballroom and his voice and the face of the girl in the booth last night. He growled at the memory. He'd offered that kid a chance. The kid didn't bother to come by—so what? The wires in his leg were striking up the pain.

'He'll change his name to *what*?' Oscar snapped.

'To Glen Dart.'

She smiled radiantly, and beside her the new creation levered with his forefinger at the nut particles lodged in his unspectacular teeth. Oscar leaned on his stick. His fury bore it into the white rug among the peanut shells, as the pain zagged up to the rods in his throat.

'What's wrong with the name he already has?'

Mrs Seldon Redman waved away this one priceless possession with charm-burdened fingers. She had directed, too, the career of her late husband. That his music proved to be eternal light was fortunate—under her vivacious tutelage, the body had quickly perished. And she served on the Ladies' Committee at the Hermitage, the Andrew Jackson home.

'Well, I think "Glen Dart" is reahlly awfully attractive and becoming and sweet. Junior has decided he wants to get across to—you know, the younger kids.'

'Does he wanna sell records?'

... And Oscar's dreams had included the night Seldon died in the back of the yellow Thunderbird wearing one thin embroidered coat for the Nebraska winter; a whisky bottle delicately clutched through a paper-bag. The widow was building a château as a memorial to him, with a guitar-shaped pool.

'Well reahlly, Mr Taliaferro, I don't see how you can expect to understand. I believe,' she said sweetly, 'that Mr Bee will go just crazy about it. May I explain it to

45

you? "Glen Dart" comes from the names of Junior's two schools, Glen Munro High and Dartmouth College.'

Oscar said, 'So why didn't you name him Munro Mouth?'

It was difficult enough for him to mount the grey wood porch, never mind climb the stairs. Half-way Oscar stopped, blinded by the point lace of evening sun through a broken window screen, and cursed them and almost started down again.

His entrance into their apartment was melodramatic. The door stood half-open but would not yield without a push. When Oscar Taliaferro had pushed, no reserves remained. He toppled in, down to the grubby ruins of a couch from which, in the same instant, Charles Pinkard rose up. The kid wore no shirt; he was hairy and his face stupid with daytime sleep.

For a while Oscar sat and regarded the black sharkskin covering the bones of his knees. Then, furiously, he pulled a book from underneath him—Gibbon's *Decline and Fall of the Roman Empire.*

They had opened up again for him, he saw contemptuously—he could remember what freezing wings used to fly out from certain Hollywood enclaves at the stranger's approach. But nobody explained why that appointment at the office had not been kept; indeed, his coming appeared to give no particular surprise. Charles Pinkard retired to the arm of another filthy chair and sat and picked a guitar. Outside his waistband, the pallid life-belt of flesh somehow appalled Oscar more than all the pleated tonnage of Buzzy Bee. The girl came in from the next room.

'What's your name?' Oscar panted at her.

'Jody,' she answered lightly. 'Uh uh—really it's Jo Ann.'

In a dress, without beehive or thickened eyes, she was

frighteningly young. The flesh on her bare legs and arms sparkled like sandpaper.

'Jo Ann used to work in the movie-theatre on Blue Grass Boulevard,' Rock Rivers said musically from the table.

'I'm glad you told me that,' said Oscar.

Rock Rivers got up, intercepted the girl and swiftly took from her a bundle of colourless rags—his newly-washed underwear. In a carefree way he threw it towards the battered silhouette of a portmanteau. He crossed the dreadful room again in the rhythmic, toe-pointing way that results from wearing the same clothes all the time.

'See my bed?' He had crouched down like a wrangler beside Oscar, who quickly moved a leg.

'Bed?'

Rock Rivers indicated a portion of the linoleum. His face wore a steadfast expression intimating 'I've slept rough before under the stars'. He lifted the piece of hair back onto his forehead.

Despite a fan that sprayed noisily in its box, the room was stifling. From the good air far away floated the desolate pup of a steel guitar. 'This is a convenient apartment,' Oscar said.

'"Convenient"!' The girls eyes made half-moons, as when she had spoken of the Ancient Romans. She was nestling against the chair into Charles Pinkard's hip; her face shone upward welcoming even the smoke out of his nose.

'Gee, you know that next-door apartment all boarded and shuttered! When I think of the dark room the other side of our wall—wow, I just lie wakeful all night with the letter-opener in my hand!'

Rock Rivers said quietly, 'Sir, are you familiar with a radio-show by a deejay named King Crab?'

'Charles, tell me why you didn't come by the office today like you said.'

47

Oscar rapped out the question half-humorously, giving him a chance—the cops; the car broke down. Charles Pinkard merely swallowed and grinned; fooling, not looking, he produced a wire-tripping splendid ascent on the keyboard of his guitar, and still did not answer Oscar's question.

'C'mon, Charles; you thought maybe I was some kinda faggot here.'

'Nuh.' He snickered.

'You thought I was some kinda faggot after your little raspberry.'

'—Sir.'

Rock Rivers lifted his face up in a dolphin's wonder, despite the glare that Oscar turned on him.

'Sir, you referred last night to the benefits of education. Well, there was a whole bunch of editorials on the King Crab Show.'

His thick, middle-aged legs bulged fearfully as he leaned back to bring his coat from the kitchen-chair. He opened his pocket-book.

'I wrote all of 'em down,' he said quietly. 'The ones that were meaningful to me.' The hair hung beside his face as he proffered some clasped bits of card. 'Please. You don't have to read all of it.'

The handwriting was the kind shared by old men and lunatics.

Always act the part of the man you would like to be. Knock and the door will be opened.

'It was a course for young sales executives,' Rock Rivers explained.

'I see,' said Oscar.

Let imagination soar. Let [indecipherable] *I can do anything that I really want to do.*

My ambition. To be as great an entertainer as Seldon Redman.

Replacing his spectacles in his breast-pocket, Oscar

regarded the man who crouched beside him.

'You are a piece of shit,' he said tonelessly.

His eye returned to the body of Charles Pinkard—stale, gristly-black, yet she rested in a warm hollow of it, a curl beside her ear unrolled like a shaving of butter. But it was something in the reflection of the guitar which had engaged Oscar's attention. He stared so concentratedly at it that even Pinkard reacted. Unslinging the guitar he held it out by the neck. The lump in his throat rose with amusement.

'Guess a person musta trod on it.'

The face of the guitar was splintered into distinct boards. Oscar got up.

He rose in such injudicious haste that for an instant his stick jabbed and bent like a water-diviner as if Rock Rivers was not there. His face pressed down into his collar-rim as if he was choking; which he was. Choking suddenly in under-arm smells of failure.

Charles Pinkard watched. With sleepy eyes he said, 'Uh uh! Man's mad at us all, hon.'

'Huh?' Her mouth dropped like a child's.

'You make me sick,' Oscar said.

'S'only a old guitar,' he muttered.

'How'd you ever find us?' she asked.

'Blowin' smoke up our butts,' his lips on her forehead said.

'Oh, you don't have to leave right now—'

As she spoke, Oscar could see that she was ill. And he remembered where he had seen her before; or where he had seen her eyes before; dull with sickness like berries. It was in that ballroom in Rockaway. The girl who had danced in his Dance-Marathon. The girl who was dancing to death.

'That's awful,' Oscar said, to the apartment.

He turned and went downstairs, unassisted.

The Sapphires

The Trouville talent contest was between performances of its Sunday double-horror programme, so before playing, Tony Pretty and I had to wait behind the screen for a monster to die; a giant Roc. It flung from it helicopters, tanks, armies, but was at last successfully bombed with dry-ice, I think. We watched it all reversed in soft, vast tones. Meanwhile Tony's nerves increased, though he claimed to have appeared on many stages more important than the Trouville. On his chin, pimples arose like trout in May. He whispered, 'I thought we was going to wear the same *colour*.'

The cinema manager inquired how he should announce us. We argued. Tony said we were 'The Orioles'. By this name we had played our first engagement together, strumming our guitars for a game of musical bumps at a Catholic children's social, but the sound of it now filled me with embarrassment. It seemed so absolutely the creation of Tony Pretty; of his shrill voice, his murmurating complexion, that greasy sheaf of hair which all but o'ertoppled him. So we struggled with alternatives as, on the screen all around us, the giant Roc at last subsided uttering distant, slightly piteous shrieks.

'How about "The Clubmen"?'

'No,' he said. 'How about "The Devils"?'

We must intimate strength and tempest and men not fully responsible for their emotions: this, in 1959, was how to be fatally attractive. Tony was seventeen, two years older than me. He wore a bootlace tie against a dirty white shirt, his black rayon trousers clutching his waist like the drawstrings of a spongebag. By arriving in my rust-coloured pullover, it was true I had broken faith about dressing approximately alike. In those days I very much hoped to be mistaken for a country gentleman's son.

'What about "The Rockefellers"?'

'All right, but it's Rockfellers"', he contradicted.

'No it's not.'

'Look, it *is*!'

We were announced as "The Rocking Fellers". We didn't win—the other contestant did, a fat boy from Newport who mimed to a Jerry Lee Lewis record. Nor, I think, were we applauded though, as we walked onstage, a voice from the darkness said, 'I *thought* it was going to be those two.' All I remember was how it felt out there, bedded in empty, limitless maroon, like living in a bruise when it begins to thrill, I could have stayed there, staring upwards, for ever. It was Tony Pretty's voice that brought me back to business. He exclaimed 'Yeah, let's go!' and set off in one of his frightful chord-solos.

At school I was not musical, nobody was. Three classes were put in the Assembly Hall together, making a din which fatigued even *ourselves*. Presently Mr du Lusignan arrived; a man over eighty, wearing a flying-helmet and a World War Two Canadian officer's sheepskin jacket, its white fleece huskily swaggering about his nodding, ancient, mottled, freckled head. He was not a music-teacher but—I cannot explain this—an engraver.

Having rapidly distributed sheet-music, Mr du

Lusignan's helmet withdrew behind an upright piano like a wrecked billiard-table standing on its side. He did not show us how to read the music nor in any way seek to persuade us it might be related to the thrash of wires dimly audible through the piano's damaged fabric. That was the art. The discipline so necessary to its fulfilment was kept by the bald little brute in a naval rating's vest who taught P.T. Upon wonderfully soft, clean plimsolls he danced about the aisles, cutting at malefactors with a whistle on a rope. The insistent malefactor he could raise to a standing position on a chair, lifting by no other point of leverage than the head.

When the noise reached a cataract, occasionally one might turn and apprehend the headmaster himself, coming by elaborate Granny's footsteps from the rear doors of the hall. His knuckles descended into the soft part of the skull. Another boy was lifted from his chair by just his head. And once or twice, from behind the piano a withered countenance, adorned by the hanging chin-straps of the careless flying-ace, would rise into view, survey us all as if he had trodden in a cowpat, then vanish once more by depression of another incomprehensible chord. And meanwhile, somewhere, a beautiful galleon that made melodies and calmed pain sailed ever wider of our grasp.

Certain of us met, however, in the Junior School Cloakroom to look at a guitar-catalogue belonging to Tozer. This was a custom not without danger of misrepresentation; and when the catalogue was discovered, it might just as well have been a dirty book. I still wonder how many people were stopped from taking up the guitar by a widely subscribed notion then that they were objects of depravity—my father, I know, suspected they were. As for the sexual mark on them, it may have been justified. In the beginning of Rock and Roll, they certainly were as unavailable to most adolescents as a woman. Simple ownership of the catalogue imparted to Tozer something of the showman. We languished after its photographs: some of the accompanying phrases—'warm responses', 'tooled head', 'mother-of-pearl inlay with blonde sunburst finish'—seemed to enter the very disordering of our glands.

That I should have been first to obtain an actual guitar and supplant the theoretical prestige of Tozer, was as typical of my situation as the disgraceful school uniform I wore. My father took me upstairs to the kitchens at the end of Seaview Pier, where he was in business, and, with a shrug, said, 'There you are, Ian— it's yours.' It was leaning against the fish-fryer. In its brown case it looked very like one of his own wrapped fowling-guns; occasional sights of which had brought my heart to an unnecessary standstill of expectation for at least the past year.

My father did not look happy. His face intimated capitulation once again to a weak and wild youth created expressly, just as my mother was, to force honest men into receivership. He must have been fatigued by all the leaflets I had put in his way during that year without ever mentioning the subject face-to-face: also he believed, with some justification, I suppose, that I would neglect a guitar in the same way as I had neglected my bicycle.

When I took it from the case it was thrilling, that day and always. You first liberated the roundness of it by unzipping a section at the bottom. Then, as the neck emerged from its sleeve, the plastic brushed the curly ends of strings about the tuning-pegs, rippling them like a harp. It altered my existence, you see, because anything will look better if it is supplementary; if you can say, '*And* I've got a pair of shoes.' My father's manner continued pessimistic, as a man who sees fresh difficulties, not a few of them sexual; but then and for a long time he filled my life in the most impressive way a parent can; as an impresario.

I must explain that what he did at the end of Seaview Pier was catering. More particularly, it was attempting to turn a quick penny out of thousands of holiday-makers deposited there by ferries from the mainland each summer weekend, and out of thousands more, queuing, queuing to go back. In all he spent twelve years trying to turn that quick penny.

His premises were a pink and grey pleasure-dome, inlaid with stained glass at the rims and crown and other incongruous places, named The Casino. It had been built by the Victorians to accommodate pierrot-shows but as soon as it was complete, they must have realized. Monstrously too draughty and grand, even by the disproportions of seaside Gothic, for any human activity that could possibly take place within, it rose like a disengaged, badly redecorated bit of Moscow at the head of a pier not otherwise adapted for pleasure of any sort. The pier was three-quarters of a mile long: an iron tramway ran down it, and steam-trains.

Inside the Casino, it was gloomy at midsummer. Even my father's ingenuity could never light that dome prop-erly; it remained ever slumbrous with dust, perhaps with memories of Royal yachts it had glimpsed through its coloured glass windows. His opportunities, in this vasty shadow, were confined to the floor, the stage and an encircling balcony. Yet from these, in twelve years he forced to a semblance of life, if not actual solvency, a café, a pin-table saloon, a roller-skating rink—during operation of which he briefly ran away with the instruc-tress—a Tea Dance (oh, iron and barnacle Tea Dance!) and, for one truly courageous epoch, a restaurant. After that, he changed it to a self-service cafeteria, but spectres of the wonderful, terrible thefts committed by the restaurant-staff continued to twitter at him out of the air. By now he was living there too, in rooms behind the stage, improvised from the narrow passageway in which Edwardian pierrots had once donned their ruffles and their flounces. The roller-skating instructress lived with him. Like almost every couple who ever eloped from the Isle of Wight, they got only as far as Portsmouth.

On the hazy days, the ferries slouched over the green waters from Spithead. I believe they actually used to clink, like bottles and base coinage. They brought more than enough people and push-chairs and orange-peel to fill the dome up to its crown. They were so full that they leaned over perilously while coming alongside; but waiting for them were steam-trains, don't forget, and the tramway which banged forth and back into the sparkling sun. It was like trying to divert the flight of the lemming. My father waited in an empty dome. Occasionally, a customer came in.

But no quick penny was ever pursued with a greater steadfastness. He was mechanically-gifted—the enduring disharmony between us sprang from my utter failure in that direction. Every new thing the floor of the Casino struggled to become was his own work; assisted only by an electric-drill, a tongue pressed at the channel of his upper-lip, and unnumbered screws, rings, nuts and other mysteries which he catalogued in Gold Block tobacco-tins and which I, should I but touch them, must disarrange or destroy.

For the self-service cafeteria—note the formality of the diction of his mass-catering—he made counters from disused chests-of-drawers, and a pay-desk which ran, with somewhat too much alacrity, on castors. My father loved castors; I have known him apply them to a rocking-chair. And he maintained by himself every one of the two hundred slot-machines—many of which he could have sold to museums later, if he had kept them—clinking through the grey-blue summer with a fleece of keys over his slightly rounded shoulders that gave him the appearance of some pearly-king fearfully tarnished.

Each empty cigarette-packet must needs have the sketch by him for some or other moving part or elevating mechanism on its white inside. And he created public-address systems by which to announce to the ferries the treats he had gloomily prepared for them. He devised systems of one-way glass for invigilation of the employees he so loathed and mistrusted and made prosperous. All winter there was hammering throughout the dome—yet as much as the lower spaces were re-papered and re-arranged, the great dome remained above, as in sleep, with its glimmer of stained-glass at the very top.

And summer after summer, while men of smaller education, who did not do crossword-puzzles or wear an emblazoned ring or fish for trout, gathered fortunes to themselves and found time for golf, that obstinate quick penny turned both its faces from my father. As my mother learned to say after their divorce, he 'farted against thunder'. Certainly he was unfortunate. The one season he yielded to the ignominy of fish and chips there occurred one of the few potato-famines recorded in modern times. I wonder now if there was in him some mechanism of self-disgust; some ultimate resistance to mass catering which compelled him always to end the year no farther forward than he had begun it, still marooned at the end of the pier, paying criminal rents. On the other hand, he never did appreciate that, if you give nice food to people, they will not object to paying money for it.

My mind has quite locked out those summer seasons of his. I need not mention how it felt to be in physical terror of Saturdays. Therefore, it seems to me now that most vivid moments of my adolescence passed in the Casino in winter; in a winter sea with the sound, somewhere, of hammering; late on a Sunday afternoon, with ferries and clink of crowds and the possibility of profit all long since withdrawn into cold-weather timetables; a chill of dusty pennies and canvas covers; the black tides creaking under the pier supports; and, glowing like a fireside over the water—Southsea.

At school I became known as the boy who lived at the end of Seaview Pier. I tried to explain this was not the case.

He didn't tell me he planned to hold a Rock and Roll dance in the Casino for defence against those long winters, nor that he had invited local groups to come down to audition. Nor, on a later occasion, that in fact he had married the skating-instructress.

My guitar made even the pier in winter look good; even the occasional lonely tram that was our only contact with the land. Each night I practised on the very spot the guitar had been given to me: in the kitchens next to the fish-fryer. Suddenly, out in the dome, I heard Elvis Presley's voice. I went up to the balcony through the waitress bump-doors and looked down to the stage.

Beside the shroud of the Compton Melotone electronic organ, purchased ambitiously on credit to swell with its chords the lugubrious galas of the next season, my father was kneeling over some amplification-equipment. My view of him from above was as I most remember him: his tongue pressed earnestly upwards, his dark widow's peak of hair outlined on a forehead wrinkled by absorption in some mechanical task, his collar almost indistinguishable from his coat in shades of farming tweed. All his resources were engaged upon testing Elvis Presley—I therefore felt intrusive and incompetent to pronounce even upon that. *Teddy Bear* stopped. *I Got Stung* followed, rose upwards and was swallowed into the darkness of the dome.

60

'I say, Dad?'

On his forehead the widow's peak shifted a little with exasperation.

'Elvis Presley's jolly good, you know.'

Everything I said to him, when I thought about it later, seemed to sound girlish.

He looked up. In contempt or in anger, he stared. His face slightly quivered.

'Oh,' he said. 'Thank you very much for telling me or I never would have known.'

He refused to discuss his preparations but, in my tremblings of over-excitement, I could not be prevented from witnessing them. I lived then at my grandmother's; his ruling, however, was that all hours between school and bedtime must be spent at the Casino. Ostensibly the reason was 'homework' but you cannot do homework in a dome; it sprang out of a more complex assumption, that the previous summer I had been guilty of 'oggling' one of the still-room maids. Note again the formality of language. I had ogled no one; but from my earliest childhood, together with the comminglings of chip-fat and pennies, a sexual odour hung on the pier, as incomprehensible to me as it was vital in the passage of my father's fortunes.

I was excited because, through this enchainment to a fish-fryer, I had as yet been unable to let the Isle of Wight know that I possessed a guitar—and now, too, an amplifier. Not the least of mysteries in my father were the moments at which he would part with money. The Compton Melotone electronic organ was bought —or its purchase commenced—at the very nadir of the Casino's history. It was when nearest to liquidation that he always seemed to be contemplating major improvements. He was also extremely generous to casual acquaintances. From paying pounds for whisky for them he would turn and intimate that it was precisely my request

for a new PT singlet which must bankrupt him finally—
yet he got me the amplifier. I don't understand.

It was made by Elpico, the size of a fairly large book.
Its capacity was five watts. Consider that a modern
band's equipment may call up three or four thousand
watts; then you may imagine the piping of this little
speaker, but alone in the kitchen, I was transfixed by it,
borne up as on the backs of charging steers. Also it
elicited from him his first reaction of any sort towards
my playing. In the evening without warning, for one
could never hear his approach, the widow's peak, thrust
forward, would look around the kitchen door. What he
generally said was, 'Clang, clang, clang.'

I was sure the audition was to be tonight. I had
defied the ban on going home first to change from my
school-clothes, and dressed as closely to a guitarist as I
could, in black trousers ironed so vehemently, they
twinkled like sharkskin. Beside the fish-fryer I stood,
flying high to the limit of the five watts, playing each
trick I knew over again and again until my finger-ends
were gashed with black reflections of the strings: the
idea being that the auditioning groups, when they
arrived, should pause and hear upstairs, a genius.

I stopped playing. There was a noise in the entrance-
hall, the bolts of the main doors being drawn, my father
speaking cordially to someone. From the stage the amp-
lification equipment—basis of his public-address system
to the heedless summer ferries—uttered a shriek, then
grew quiet save for the huge expectancy of the live mike.
Husked by embarrassment, a shrill voice said 'One-two'.
I could bear it no longer.

The lips of the dome were lit by the strings of coloured
carnival bulbs, never as a rule turned on in winter,
and by the red and blue footlights; their jollity and
softness pricking out the chill, warming the lips of the
dome, making even the hunger and slop of the encircling

waters seem nice, as if one was snug in the ballroom of an ocean-liner. On the stage, before the shrouded Compton Melotone organ, were a group of five.

Four of them wore pale blue shirts and navy trousers; my eye flew at once, however, to the fifth who, as leader, displayed these colours in reverse, and seemed to represent everything I had ever wished for myself. He was little and thin-waisted. By the earnest angle of his sheaf of hair over the guitar I imagined some sixth-former of diabolical cleverness at a mixed school where every girl held him in awe. I longed to be held in awe by girls. His complexion appeared scrubbed pink, and I pictured the good home he came from, with never a fear of Saturdays. Indeed, his life seemed all miracles. On the cord round his neck, he wore something I had only ever seen in the pages of Tozer's catalogue at school. A guitar with one shoulder carved away; in order that brilliant fingers might ascend to the smallest, hardest figures of the keyboard.

The Sapphires. They began to play—I watched over the balcony, careful to remain out of sight of the widow's peak below on the tenderly-lit dance-floor. In my isolation from, among other things, the radio, I had never heard before what they were rehearsing: *Rebel Rouser*. It was merely first of a dynasty of elementary tunes played all on the bass-notes of a guitar. For years, indifferent performers clung to it or its imitations rather as plain cooks use suet; but that night its deep throat stilled even the echo in the dome. Later on, next to the fish-fryer, I worked out quite easily how to do it—no one had intended it should be inaccessible to beginners. In fact it could be played without moving the fingers far from the E Major chord-shape. You then repeated groups of notes corresponding around the F and so on to G and A; excitement and wild saxes increasing with this ascent.

But in rehearsal the leader of The Sapphires showed the perfectionism I had also guessed of him. From the balcony all of it sounded perfect to me, and looked breathtaking. They had an electric guitar for rhythm as well as for his solos. They had, not a snare-drum, but a full, twinkling set; no tea-chest and broom but the incarnation of an adult double bass, played by a tall person whose voice boomed in my hearing from time to time. Yet the leader seemed to detect some fault. He repeatedly played the E phrase, struck the change to F, then stopped them. Afterwards I discovered that Tony Pretty had only mastered that first part of *Rebel Rouser* and could proceed no farther.

I now have to account for the continuing presence of Tony Pretty among us at the end of the pier, and can do so only by stating brutally a further aspect of my father, which may also explain why he was neither able to accumulate funds nor instil in us related to him by blood, any lasting confidence. He was born to be a leader of men who see it judicious not to answer back.

All his inclinations—apart from those gratified by the skating-instructress—were towards genteel masculinity; the solitary pursuits consequent upon rural private means, such as fly-fishing and wildfowling, with socialising only for purposes of limitless celebration. He wore, as I have said, a ring with a coat-of-arms on it, inscribed 'Press Forward' and dull, gentleman farmer tweeds with leather piping. His RAF shield hung on the wall of the tiny pierrots' dressing-room which he inhabited with the skating-instructress and her collection of evening-shoes. And sometimes in the narrow passageway behind the stage, vibrating with pumps from the Compton Melotone electronic organ or juddering in the shoulder of angry seas, one might come across—but never dare touch—other fragments from an earlier life of leather-gaiters and pipe-tobacco: a salmon-net or bandolier of orange cartridges or volume of dressed Terry's Terror or Tupp's Indispensable dry-flies.

I am certain he envisioned that quick penny as a fishing beat on the Avon. He also preserved the assumption of the post-war years, gratified in so many thousand less conscientious cases, that society owed him a living. Instead, he gained the kingdom that he despised—a Shanghai of all the scum and worthlessness of the seaside August. He was liege to, and considered finely educated by, rogue-chefs, kitchen-porters, sexually over-alert female electronic-organists (of which four were variously employed, one with a cankered ear) and tram-drivers, lobster-poachers, pierhead ticket-clerks, open-air photographers, seasonal newspaper vendors, Trinity House pilots, fat women whose presence I cannot explain, but if you laid a hand unsuspectingly on a bar-stool, they would come and sit down on it; draymen, wholesalers of balloons, funny hats and squeakers and, oh, the 'casual staff'!

In the season I have known upwards of sixty to work in the Casino; mainly in the kitchens where, believe me, the object of their labours was anything but casual. While the honest minority found their every movement invigilated by my father's grim jaw—their bags submitted to lightning checks—their smallest gestures spied on through one-way glass and ill-concealed peepholes—the dishonest remainder tranquilly prospered. Indeed, they formed the habit of meeting their friends and relations every Friday night in a pub on the Esplanade, when all would receive their groceries for the week. To the end of his life my father would repeat this story himself in an appalled voice with eyes staring, with lips fatigued by outrage; yet still regarding it as an irreversible situation which he might have read about. 'And if

65

they couldn't steal butter,' he used to say, 'they *grumbled!'*

In winter, too, notwithstanding an impression that each day might be our last, there were always people hanging about; now there was Tony Pretty. My father did not tell me he had joined the Casino employees. I first grew aware of his company in the small bar which, from September to May, served as our living-room. It was opened every evening the year round, but the idea was not for people to come in, even had there been people to attempt this. At the bend of the counter stood a television set and small electric fire: near the filaments of the latter, my father, the skating-instructress —and now Tony Pretty—would huddle and eat the Marmite sandwiches that formed our diet in the troublesome months, as the pier swayed in unquiet sea, watching quiz shows on television.

Tony, despite the grandness of his education, did not seem to do much. I can remember him steadying the ladders on which my father stood. It took time to realize that his actual status at the Casino was friend of mine. Although two years older than me, he quickly became subject to most of the laws regulating my existence—laws usually concerned with stopping things that had started. He was there every evening. Later, to my great awe, he would join me for guitar-practice in the kitchens next to the fish-fryer; he hadn't an amplifier at the moment, so I always let him use the Elpico.

My first impression of him, earnest with a spray of hair over that spellbinding guitar, had been cut from all the current legends. But his hair was dyed. The pinkness and pouting of his full face, his small, sharp nose, proved, at close quarters, to be an occupation of the worst case of spots it is possible to imagine without allusions to an aerial view of the crowd on Derby Day. His voice, in both speech and song, had discernible elements of the boy soprano. Straight away he told me that, in the Advanced Level GCE, he had received ninety-eight per cent for music, and added self-consciously, 'highest honours'. This I discovered to be exaggeration, together with much else of what he said. It also was revealed that, on the very night of the audition, he had been expelled from The Sapphires for qualities not visible from the balcony—arrogance and want of hygiene.

With the same catch of self-loathing which accompanied his feats of summer showmanship, such as refereeing Gala night cockle-eating contests, my father introduced the only Rock group ever to perform live at the Casino's winter 'session', as he called it. Not The Sapphires— they had disbanded around Tony—but a standoffish grammar school quartet named Les Paysans whose guitars were made from stolen materials by a friend in an aircraft factory. The quick penny was not forthcoming from the Rock and Roll dance: my father capitulated to that once. By the next week, Les Paysans had been dismissed, the microphones removed from the stage, two-thirds of the lights switched off and a jukebox installed for which the dancers themselves had to pay. The only time he emerged from the little front-bar was to adjust this jukebox when it had been attacked.

The 'session', a word which is the quintessence of my father's voice, became, since he could not be bothered to terminate it, a bi-weekly affair. On Wednesdays, perhaps half a dozen people came, of whom one or two couples fed the jukebox and jived. The rest sat in shadow around the dance-floor, occasionally flicking the red buttons of their cigarettes in bouncing flashes among the dancers' legs. Then—Saturday night.

The motor-cycles ripped down the pier, knocking aside the careful devices of all-night fishermen, squashing bait. On the pierhead, the glass of weighing-machines and automatic telescopes and deckchair arsenals was smashed; the pipeclayed lifebelts tossed into the sea. And that impassive pavilion, that slumbrous dome for the first time in its life very nearly awoke.

The dance-floor, where in the past my father had sometimes ferociously quickstepped to encourage the others, where the skating-instructress had performed the Mohawk, where my family had in fact broken up all on roller-skates, where people scoring a million at pinball had been entitled to a prize of one toffee, where ton upon ton of powder potato, processed peas and vacuous meat-pie had been consumed, an infinity of horrible food sold but no penny yielded up save with excruciating reluct-ance—this floor was now a shallow lake of the ullage of brown ale. What trampled in it, this way and that, was like nothing so much as some army of revolution, dreadfully bewildered. Hundreds of beer-crazed youths in sweaters pushed up to the elbow, with Boston hair, tattooed wrists, crumpled ears, not dancing—for the jukebox was obliterated—but, by the cruel lights under the dome, moving in one ghastly Conga: a thunder of motor-cycle boots that was club-footed and frightening.

To allay breakage, my father used wood battening to nail all the chairs together in files of thirty. This pro-moted the breaking of them to thirty at a time. Other-wise he remained out of earshot in the bar, watching the quiz-shows. Each new evasion by the quick penny could be ascribed to forces beyond his control—to the casual staff, the Government, the pier-authorities or, in the case of the 'session', to a gang of toughs from Newport called the Brodies. My father's belief in them as saboteurs continued, even after one night their whole motorcade struck a van, and six out of eight Brodies perished.

He was steadfast in one thing, however—restricting me. Rock and Roll dancing was his affair, transacted from his (this phrase is also redolent of him) *private-office*, and therefore it could have nothing to do with me, I must mind my own business. On Saturday nights as the dome shook, I was forbidden to come out of the kitchens, but sometimes Tony and I would steal through the bump doors and gaze upon the hordes, rather like inquisitive Tsarists in 1916.

If my father's purpose was to shield me from the sight of primitive passions—from 'oggling'—this was unattainable. You went out on the pierhead, and every angle of its fantail railingwork, the crevices of the quay, the darkened bench along the tramway-station; all darkness was intense with movement, with snorting and breathing and the brightening of cigarettes; or an occasional glimmer of shirt-tails as, in the wildness of the embrace, someone's coat rode up his back.

From the balcony I became, for the first time, aware of legs. They belonged to a girl who wore white, pointed shoes. For that time of bouffants and lacquer she had her hair cut unnaturally short: she was somewhat bucktoothed. Yet she seemed, even in the ugly shifts of the Saturday crowd, to preserve an exclusive, forbidding sexuality, as if her father might be a hangman. Even the Brodie with the crumpled ear would ask her formally to jive, and smile if she refused. Never in my sight was she wetted with beer or caught in any girl-fights, which would occasionally kick stocking gaps in the formation —and Tony Pretty said he had been alone with her once, in her sitting-room. At this, my face froze. What was she like?

He looked thoughtful. No girl, as I understood, had ever been able to withstand him; he had 'had it' five times. Currently the most impressive of his spots, glowing like a waxed-tile, almost completely covered the tip of his nose. At length he answered:

'As cold as ice.'

His girl friend at that time was Josie. Excess flesh hung in rails over her shoes and pressed her cheeks up together as if by unseen hands. Nonetheless, she always dressed in a tight and complicated way that, taken with a way she had of posing at the door with one toe pointed, puts me in mind now of the better-known portraits of Louis XIV.

As we practised, with the Elpico and a tape-recorder Tony was buying, Josie sat up in the cold kitchen with us, singing along in an admiration I found most heartening. Then at a certain point, Tony would rise and put out the light. I sat on in the darkness, playing to myself all I could remember of his tricks, looking at the twin eyes of the cigarettes the lovers had set at the edge of the spare-chair. And at the grey window, Tony's meagre profile merged with Josie's stout one; there were noises, a cough, sometimes the protest, 'No-o-o Tone, I haven't got the right things on!'

He had the brutality of anaemia in him; that perverse grinning with small mammal eyes which makes you want to pick somebody up and shake them. I provoked it sometimes by mistakes in chord-changes, and to Josie he could be vile. Her other name was Hunnybun. She was sweet tempered, our first fan and she made me feel talented. Tony had detected her weakness. Like most fat girls she acted the part of a frail little thing, the merest leaf, played by tempestuous emotion. One night we were recording the Rick Nelson song *Lonesome Town*, with Josie singing along. Tony started to extemporise words to it containing references, which only she understood, to a former love-affair of his. The tape still exists somewhere. At a point in it, Tony's voice breaks off—there is a sharp cry of distress, the clap of a hand-bag-catch, and the sound of the kitchen-door slamming upon heavy-howitzer tears.

There were also nights as if we were drunk: the

70

two of us, weak with laughter at raspberries we had recorded, the whole world throbbing in the rosy agony of our fingers, might not stop playing until past eleven o'clock.

To get out we had to go through the bar where at that hour my father would be having supper. His suppers, more than anything, gave me a feeling all of us were adrift on Seaview Pier by some ghastly slip in the gearboxes of Time. At the height of his difficulties, he remained the type of man who has his own personal and private table-delicacies. He would be eating hand of pork, belly of pork and brawn and pickled walnuts, foods from an Oxfordshire inn-garden in the sunshine before the war, while outside, the wind mourned round the scaffold in the sea and the face of an all-night fisherman appeared like a ghost's at the glass bar-door.

As a rule I would be told off for prodigality with the Elpico's five watts. In those days the mark of my familiarity with anyone was that they had seen me abused by my father. 'This isn't a land o' plenty any more, Ian, you know,' he used to say contemptuously. Yet one was never sure—his expansiveness at other times might include hugging and kissing me; stories of his RAF Squadron or great pre-war shooting-hampers; renewal of his promise to buy me a suit. It was what always prevented my attitude to him from clarifying beyond a vague unease. Precisely at the moment I was confident of thoroughly disliking him, he perversely won my confidence all over again.

On this night he told us to stop practising and come down and have a drink. That was the first time in my life I ever was allowed to taste light-ale, though for two summers past I'd worked behind various of the Casino's bars. Tony Pretty and I, still wearing our guitars round our necks, and he and his second wife—for so the skating-instructress had by now been transformed—all

71

sat in the brilliantly-lit, deserted bar, watching a quiz-show on television. Then my father asked, 'Well, do you intend earning your living from your guitars or what?'

Tony said, 'Yeh.' I said I didn't know, but made it 'Yes'. To be truthful, in the head-dream of the light-ale and his sudden radiance towards us, I was transfixed all over again by hopes in vague shapes of his infinite powers of arrangement and patronage and subsidy; the pier stood motionless in the sea for a moment. Then, all he said was, why didn't we play something for them?

We did the Buddy Holly song *Well All Right*; the soprano and repetitive half-chords of Tony Pretty replacing the inflection and beating Flamenco of the original. As we were playing, the face of an all-night fisherman came to the bar-doors, rattled them and disappeared. Before we had quite finished, my father's wife arose and began to lay out at the end of the bar the paper bags containing his hand of pork and belly of pork, and the big caterer's jar of yellow pickle. We stopped: for a while he sat in an attitude of engineering thought, pulling at his lower lip with both thumbs.

'Yes...' he said.

'But Ian, I wish you'd play something we could appreciate.'

This was his wife, the former skating-instructress, making one of her rare essays into speech. I only ever really picture her from the days of the roller-rink: large, slightly chilly legs from a short pleated skirt disappearing into white skating-boots. My mother's instructions were that she was wicked but her treatment of me, or 'currying favour' as my mother expressed it, always showed the greatest long-suffering especially as, I am ashamed to say, I still pretended to be too wounded and proud of the family name to talk much to her. She came from Birmingham, had a little mouth, collected coloured shoes. Her abiding virtue was that, all through those summers, she stuck by him. He set store by her views in theatrical matters, too, for she had also once been a semi-professional acrobatic dancer. 'I used to love Al Bowlly's singing,' she added reminiscently.

Now it happened that for several days I had been away from school with 'flu. Compelled, as always, to pass my time in the bracing airways of the Casino, I had occupied it with a note-for-note transposition to acoustic-guitar of *The Lady is a Tramp* which I know is a boring song—I know. But for the learner it has the advantage of being easy to follow by ear, at the same time affording one or two satisfactory movements across the keyboard where most of your early solo exercises go only up and down. Therefore I offered to play *The Lady is a Tramp*.

This meant Tony must accompany—the first time I had so much as hinted challenge of the order by which he was soloist and master and I the supplicant pupil. He didn't want to, but probably concluded it was on my goodwill that his future suppers of hand of pork and belly of pork depended. We started again. It came to me, suddenly, what it was like to play lead-guitar. *'And,'* I thought, 'I've got a light-ale.' The sea wind caught the pier, almost whirling it from its stilts. Tony kept up, doing chords. My father and his wife arose. With the slight squash of his noiseless shoes on the lino, around the desolate bar they began to dance the Quickstep.

Sometimes he would even allow us to use the stage and microphones. Our voices ascending to the lost scales of the dome actually sounded as if we could sing. It was on one such munificent night that Tony saw a face he recognized at the ballroom windows, and went and admitted it through the doors from the tram-station. Across the dance-floor walked somebody tall, wearing a long blue jacket, and bony in the way that suggests a rod held crookedly through the shoulders. Then I realized I'd seen him before; playing double-bass in The Sapphires the night they first came down to audition.

His name was 'Spud' Hayter. He addressed me directly by name; something I have always found hard to resist. He'd seen the light in the Casino while all-night fishing with his Dad. Since the dissolution of The Sapphires, apparently he had joined a new group: what if he should offer, as I dared not think, to practise with us? But in his deep voice he rapidly did better than that. Through a grin I heard him say to Tony, 'Oi'll come in with you, Nipper.'

Spud, too, wore his hair in a sheaf, but unlike Tony's his was assiduously combed and clean. A barber's apprentice at Ventnor, Spud's life seemed composed of all agreeable things like hair spray and surgical rubber. His eyes humorously stood out, particularly when he looked at Tony, and with his deep, intimate Isle of Wight voice he had formed a private collection of phrases which he would utter very rapidly and discreetly. Offering me a piece of chewing-gum, he said, 'Have you seen Tony's Dad, Ian? Yeh—queer as a snake he is, Ian, queer as a snake and that's a fact, Ian. Walks along as though he's shit hisself, he does, Ian. Queerasasnake!'

Scarcely any groups at that time owned bass-guitars—some indeed, outside London, still clung to the shameful traps of broom and tea-chest from the days of Skiffle. A full-grown double bass such as Spud had acquired slightly shopworn, helped by a massive loan from an aunty in Cowes, made an astonishing difference when it joined our combined guitars' faint tin. Suddenly we felt as if we played with every exit covered, and our backs against a good, strong wall.

Of course, in The Sapphires, Spud had not cared for Tony Pretty much. Even at their greatest triumphs, he told me, Tony's behaviour had proved officious. But

74

what I never understood was why, despising him, Spud should have chosen to make so much of me. I can now see how much Tony and I were of a type—both of us fearful pretenders fated to be feeble bystanders. And our fathers were also of a type, despite the anxiety of Mr Pretty's walk. He, too, pursued a quick penny, in a guest-house at the top of town, smelling of gravy and ferrets, whereas Spud's Dad was dignified by skill and wages. The Saturdays we all feared, Spud's Dad spent in a villa facing the police-station, at his ease.

Spud showed absolutely no reticence, in front of either his father or mine. I was astonished to find myself allowed to leave the pier with him on Sunday afternoons. It was from Spud I learned to drink Boilermakers, smoke cigarettes, say 'What's on then?' to pairs of unaccompanied girls and take them to horror-films for the best results. Spud showed me a frog's skeleton; told me the one about the doctor and the windscreen-wipers; described a vengeance he once took by posting to his antagonist a lolly-stick dipped in dog-excrement. He had a vast acquaintanceship and was the first person I ever knew who could be *friendly* towards girls. Faces I had spied on from the balcony now received names: Norma Joliffe, Florence Niblet, Jackie Ramage, Patsy Fry. But I remained utterly tongue-tied in their presence, even when Spud literally picked me up and deposited me among the limbs of an eight-strong petting orgy on parkland covering the disused gun-emplacements at Puckpool.

Thanks to his influence over my father—whom he dared actually to chaff—I was allowed to leave the pier even on certain weeknights. Tony I saw now only when we met to practise. At Spud's insistence, he no longer sang: we did instrumental numbers with myself in the lead and Tony playing chords. I began to realize, too, that not all of his chords were perfect. That night in the bar when we were given light-ale, the white scratch-plate of his guitar had received a large cigarette-burn. In any case, though admittedly a cutaway, it wasn't *so* much of a guitar. 'Sounds loike a bloody bag o' wires,' Spud said, 'and that's a fact, Ian.' While he and I were out together I believe Tony used to sit up in the kitchens with his tape recorder, by himself as Josie had also deserted him.

Spud and I left him to make his own way to Bembridge. We were playing in The Starling Trophy; a contest for groups at a pub in Bembridge, solemnized by an actual challenge-cup. Tony had entered us because The Sapphires were the previous year's winners, and the cup was still at his house.

On a solemn and mild winter seaside night, the Esplanade was dead but for the lighted bands of our bus; the discreetly pushing sea held long lamp reflections in it, which raised up the pier on a colonnade of gold. Far down, the hooped railings and pagoda shelters vanished into mist from which a slow foghorn repeated. It might have been a dome stirring in sleep with dreams of fast pennies irrecoverably lost in the summers of long ago.

Going by bus anywhere was fun with Spud. He'd sit and point at complete strangers and if they moved, follow them with his finger, or twiddle imaginary taps at the fronts of girls' coats or, leaning close up to some harmless old couple, make a noise that was half a threat, half a yodel—'*And your old lady too!*' Also we had the double bass with us.

Arch, landlord of The Starling and impresario for the contest, belonged to a side-whisker type of publican in stiff collar and pullover, who look jovial and military but aren't and who, as well as beer, sell things such as chocolate, questionable car-radios and what Spud used to call 'nodders'. The stage on which we were to make our first appearance—if you will discount Tony Pretty and myself at the Catholic children's social and the Trouville—was merely the end of a saloon-lounge covered in framed mottoes, horsebrasses, Christmas-club particulars and the hatbands of sailors.

It was empty, we were so early, but I loved arriving anywhere with a guitar. All in fact which spoiled the intriguing spectacle of Spud and I and the double-bass at the bar, was the arrival of Tony Pretty. He wore a long grey gaberdine raincoat, belted tightly round him, as if he had just come down from Jarrow with the hunger-marchers.

He indicated his shoes.

'Like those?' he asked.

We looked.

'Ox-blood,' Tony said pompously.

'Looks loike you still got the tongues in 'em, Nipper,' was Spud's comment.

'The Cherokees are coming,' Tony announced. Against the bar I kept my tough-customer attitude, but I was prepared to give up and go home right then. In the whole Isle of Wight, the Cherokees were first to have solid electric guitars in the shapes of sharks and spears. Their soloist was a man of miracles named Chick. 'They got their own car,' Tony added pointlessly.

But it was too late to withdraw. Round the walls, the straight chairs were filling up. Our audience were Teddy-boys but, being already somewhat dated, of a placid, law-abiding sort who would sit in silence the whole night over a pint of brown ale. Each Ted had a girl friend with him of approximately one-third his size; in fact the boot-lace tie of the male gave some couples a passing resemblance to a Quaker with his little daughter. At certain moments, the Ted would briefly inquire, 'All right then?' His tiny partner nodded. They went outside, leaving their places marked. When they returned, the girl had nettle-marks on her legs or her skirt on inside-out.

The Teds had enormous respect, however, for guitarists. One of them in particular befriended us—Ebbo. He wore a black coat to the knees, picked out in squares of gold, and a tie which divided his barrel chest like the seam of a broad bean. Ebbo performed a milk-round—with a horse, Spud said—but also he possessed a remarkable singing voice. In the palm of one hand, tattooed with the words 'Mother' and 'Father', he showed me an object I took at first to be a flattened-out grey bogey.

'Know what this is, Nipper?' Ebbo inquired.

'No, I'm sorry, I don't.'

' "No, I'm sorry, I don't"?' he echoed, but not unkindly. 'Fibreglass plectrum that is, see?'

He and Spud looked over the unattached girls.

'That's Frances Hackshawe,' Spud said. 'Oi'd ask her for a jive but oi always gets such an hard on.'

'I've heard she's a practising pro,' Tony supplied. They ignored him.

'Ah—hello, Sandra Toogood! Oi've had *her* behoind the Duver for a little feel,' Spud said. Ebbo beamed at this.

'Oi bet she's heard about *moi* reputation. Oi don't reckon *she'd* take a bit of frigging.'

'And your old lady too,' Spud yodelled.

'There y'are, Tony,' Spud added unkindly. 'Friends of yours, Tony.'

A skiffle-group had just walked in.

The rest might have been dreams induced by light-ale. The Cherokees never did arrive. Our only opponents in The Starling Trophy were that skiffle-group; and its guitarist was blind and the washboard-player had two artificial legs; though by Nature's compensation, the dexterity of his fingers was very great.

The Teds seemed quite accustomed to them, how-ever; even to the way the washboard-player's torso moved in rhythm while his legs remained immobile. But, judged even to the low measure of skiffle-groups that God made whole, they were not outstanding. I can never hear Lonnie Johnson sing *Careless Love* without skin-crawlings at how they crippled that one. Their performance concluded with *Streamline Train*, which the blind guitarist started off too quickly; and the others had to grind down to its right tempo, thereby posing difficulties, if not actual hazards, to the torso of the washboard-player. They received a pleasant round of applause. Then Arch announced us:

The New Sapphires.

If my childhood on Seaview Pier led me to any philosophy at all it was that generally one is in the wrong. At The Starling that night, in front of those orderly and solemn Teds, I discovered a new sensation. The influence of two light-ales cannot, of course, be dis-counted; but there was something else in me, too; in all three of us as we played, walled round by the stomach-note of Spud's bass. In the feel of my fingers on the key-board, the apprehensiveness of my whole adolescence seemed to vanish. We sounded good, like three close friends. It might even have been skill.

Arch the landlord, in the style of the great compères, read out the names of the runners-up first. They were the skiffle-group—the Holidaytimers—who, I daresay, were pleased enough with the result. To acknowledge the applause they stood, one leaning on rubber-ended sticks, another with his eyes shut. The winners were The New Sapphires; the lampshades danced; the only moment I ever wanted, *desperately*, to see the widow's peak of my father suddenly appear round the door. Be-cause I was in the right. Because it *couldn't* sound like

79

a girl, you see. More light-ale was presented to us, in the trophy we had won. Spud and I took care not to drink from the same side of it as Tony.

Arch was at the microphone again. He'd like to ask the boys to come back and play a few more numbers. Our problem was that we only knew three, and had already done all of them. Borne up on such lightness of ale, how could that deter us?

'Uh, we've had a request,' Tony said.

'—from Spud's Mum,' I put in, and there was cheering and laughter.

'—for *El Rancho Rock* again.'

They clapped.

'—for *The Lady is a Tramp* again.'

Here there was such ecstasy that, after a consultation, we decided to try something.

'What we going to call it?' Tony whispered.

'What do you want to call it, Ian?' Spud amended; and I was inspired to reply '*The Scratcher*.'

'Uh—' Tony announced. 'Ian wrote this one.'

A voice said, 'Well played, Nipper.'

As I played *The Scratcher*, that feeling of infallibility was still in my fingers. '*And*,' I thought, 'I've got a silver cup.' I looked at Tony, playing just chords, but can't say I felt any remorse at what I'd done to him. I smiled. He smiled back.

They wouldn't let us stop. Ebbo proposed that he should sing with us, having been convinced by our brief exchange over the fibreglass plectrum that I was among the greater guitarists living. He himself had no guitar but, outside in his van, the largest, most carelessly-built amplifier I had ever seen; just a radiogram speaker supported in the timbers of a small wardrobe. When I struck an E Major through it I even got a small shock up my strings, but to strike that E Major, I would have burned.

In front of me, Ebbo's short body grew rigid. They whistled—I tremble a bit now as I did then. Ebbo slid one rubber-soled shoe a little distance from the other so that he faced the audience like a parrot. Up through his chest came, first the noise of a sink trying desperately to free itself, then, through the same tiny opening in his lips, Elvis Presley's voice, but *he* didn't move, except to tear and re-tear a cigarette-packet to bits in his fingers. Except to shake his gold-threaded cuff at me.

'Take it,' he commanded.

I took it—the solo—flying. On dry land. On my knees. A voice said, 'Well played, Nipper.'

Mister Movin

'Honey' Sweetman and the doctor watched from the drugstore across the street. By late afternoon the queues stretched already a full block either side of Frosch's Playhouse. Captain Arthur must have twenty patrol men on duty out there, fearful and white, but most of them could stand in thankful groups under the marquee; revolver butts swaggering through their graceful coat tails. One appearance by Mr Movin had been calculated to equal, in any city, a hundred police.

Leafing through the one-dollar, full-colour Mister Movin souvenir programme, the doctor exclaimed, 'Hey—remember last show he done here? When he was completely out and they thought he had a heart attack? You know what it was? Complete dehydration!'

'What'd you do?' inquired Captain Arthur, sitting down. 'Give him a salt-tablet and a bill for a hundred bucks?'

'Nope—two pints of fluids and a bill for two hundred.'

Honey's and the doctor's cheekbones had the pertness of mixed blood. Captain Arthur was of the true, heroic black, however, with features as from lustrous coal polished smooth. As he unbuttoned his uniform-tunic, a shirt of rich rust appeared between the blue. 'Doc,' he asked, 'in that brochure does it refer to Mister Movin stoppin' the Grailer riots?'

The doctor looked.

'We-ell—here it say, "Music, in Mister Movin's belief, is the only form of revolutionary communication that is non-violent." M'*hm.* Here it say, "The Colour of My Skin is a Glory Not Sin—Mister Movin's world-famous motto." Oh my!' Here the doctor's voice grew comical: his eyes expanded to their whites.

'Why heah,' the doctor intoned, 'we got a chah'min invite from de pres'dint ob de whole *U*-nited States fo' dinner at de White *House*, Wash'ton D.C.—and man, ah sho' hopes dey done got ham'n' grits down—'

'What'd Mister Movin go to the White House for?' Honey asked.

'Makin' a million dollars,' the doctor suggested. 'Man, I'm reducin' but I gotta have me a grilled cheese.'

'Stoppin' the Grailer riots,' said Captain Arthur.

'Hey, after that kid was killed outside the record store, right?'

'A building,' Captain Arthur said gravely, 'the Africa Records building. The National Guard shot a girl fifteen. Mister Movin was playin' the Astradome, Texas, that night and they networked the whole show coast-to-coast three times. He made a speech too. He said, "Now cool it—none o' you ain't about to throw your shoes in the trashcan and break up the whole street." They had tanks out, but ever'body just stayed home watchin' Mister Movin.'

'M'*hm,*' the doctor said lightly, 'and I hear tell he don't do no concert nowhere 'less he gets the popcorn franchise too.'

'And Mister Movin hats,' said Honey, who was stage-manager at Frosch's, 'and Mister Movin dolls and greasy Mister Movin pork-chop sandwiches with Mister Movin's face on 'em—'

86

'Wearin' a crown,' the doctor added.

'Lots of performers make it on eccentricity,' Captain Arthur protested, 'look at James Brown.'

'James Brown makes it on stamina and strength.'

'Doc,' said Honey, 'I heard it, Mister Movin done challenged Brother James.'

'In Atlanta, Georgia.' Occasionally the doctor smiled an obliging, dazzling smile left over from days as a soft-shoe artist. 'I'm tellin' *you*. Did he dance James Brown to *death*!'

'He is always,' Captain Arthur said, 'the complete impresario Mister Movin.'

That much was not in dispute.

'Remember the night he was brought onstage in a coffin?'

'You know what happened? He got closed in it.'

'Remember when he threw that diamond ring off the ship?'

'Remember when he wanted the red carpet out on the sidewalk?'

'And,' Honey said, 'last time he done a show here, he hadda have thirty in the band; ten Go-Go girls and— what's the name o' those guys that guard the Tower of Big Ben, England? Four of those guys he hadda have in red vests.'

'He sure got the Baby Jesus Thing,' said the doctor. 'You know? Like he really b'lieves he can walk on water.'

Captain Arthur, re-buttoning his tunic, looked solemn.

'Don't he ever make *you* feel that way, Doc, like you could?'

At that moment an enormous cockroach galloped along the rim of the booth where they were sitting. The doctor went vigorously for it with the Mister Movin brochure but, despite the blows, it reached a crevice in the wall and vanished.

'Even Mister Movin can't kill the roaches in this place,' the doctor remarked drily.

'Oh-kay,' Mr La Rosa shouts, '*on* stage! On stage ever'body, 'less anybody wants a hundred-dollar fine.' He angrily hits his side with a newspaper. 'Anybody's got no business back here, will you please— *leave!*'

Obedient to standing-orders, Mr La Rosa wears a formal suit with waistcoat, and a small Tyrolean hat. His jacket, indeed, is so sharp it has three back vents, even though his fingernails remain tipped with the filth of the road-manager's calling. This—now that Pegley has wormed above him in the organization—is Mr La Rosa's sole responsibility, hence the brusqueness of his manner. He applies the system of fines by which Mister Movin governs the road-show. Twenty dollars for dirty shoes or, for missing the bus, it could be a month's salary. Should Mr La Rosa fail to apprehend something, he himself is fined.

They stream up the iron stairs from dressing-rooms below the earth and take position behind the murmurous red curtains—a ten-piece Afro-Rock combination in gold jump-suits; two drummers; the talking-drummer; string and woodwind players in old men's tuxedos; one ladylike 'cellist in a cocktail dress. But with every musician onstage, despite Mr La Rosa's threats there are still more people in the wings than Honey Sweetman's eye can absorb at a glance. Fire Regulations are being infringed ten times over but Captain Arthur says let it go for the moment.

The backstage company, by diffusion of stage-lights, seems attractive and wonderfully alert. Mostly they are disc-jockeys from local Soul stations, wearing braid-slashed vaquero trousers, shirt collars of the height and rigidity of Regency beaux; and each, by his own account, is a boyhood friend of Mister Movin. They clown a good deal, laugh, show their new boots to one another and scrunch their hands down into boxes of Mister Movin popcorn. It is noticeable, however, that all of these close companions stay wonderfully clear of the alcove leading to the single dressing-room in the wings, where a single white man sits in a camel overcoat.

His hair hugs his cheek like silver earmuffs. He looks, in the camel coat, gentle and distinguished and fatherly until the dark scar shows across his forehead—his eyes. And until it is remarked that in none of the hamburger-joints around Frosch's Playhouse is Mister Movin's own personal and private United States Marshal ever required to pay for his order. He stands. The folds of the camel coat fall straight.

Whenever the marshal's coat straightens, it brings all of them backstage to attention; to a condition of utter silence and most fearful homage and anxiety to worship. Now Captain Arthur and two security guards advance, clearing a path from the alcove to the mouth of the wings with night-sticks rather as palms held before the Messiah; and disc-jockeys are thrust back against the brickwork like ordinary men, and beyond the curtains, they know already what is happening. An audience has animal powers of scent. Mister Movin, alone among great stars, appears at the start of his shows as well as the finish. Out there, upon the fizzing brass of the band opening one shapely dark chord is imposed, of human expectation.

The dressing-room door opened. It was the guitarist and bass-player; last of the musicians to emerge from the debriefing which Mister Movin conducted after every show. The first was now over. In the wings they had seen, from an oblique angle, one miracle.

Mr La Rosa was the only person who did not quiver

erect at any movement in the alcove. He sat with his back to it, hat saucily on his head, consuming a takeout order of Soul food.

After the two bandsmen came Mr Pegley: once more, everyone backstage came to vivid attention excepting Mr La Rosa, who licked his fingers. Mr Pegley was dressed with equal formality but his nails were clean and his hat bore a partridge feather. Between these two dapper men, loathing flew in the briefest exchange.

'Wings 'n' Things, Mr La Rosa?'

'Wings 'n' Things, Mr Pegley.'

The stage door had been left unlocked to re-admit those who went out between shows for coffee and food. From time to time, the unlit stage curtains were disturbed by an unlawful freeze of street air. Captain Arthur led another boy away down the ramp, a woolly head snuggled in a windcheater collar, and gently replaced him in the queue for the second house.

The disc-jockeys were still there. But they now neither whooped nor ate popcorn. Having expended several hours of worship in cold dust, they were still unsure if their presence had been even noted. They had begun to experience, behind their nodding collars, that thrill of fatigue which only the time sycophant understands—or stage-staff like Honey Sweetman. Honey watched the Preacher talk to the Go-Go Dancer. His folded arms tightened with desire and with resentment of the power of priests over women.

Back against the water-cooler, an Englishman looked about him with somnambulist's terror. He was waiting to speak to Mister Movin on behalf of his London music paper; an event which record-company executives in London had predicted to be the warmest certainty. Already he had waited a night and a day. He had seen Mister Movin pass by. He had expended his last clean shirt. He had shaken more inconsequential black hands, however, than the Chief Boy Scout at an International Jamboree.

'Hi, how's it goin'?' the guitarist and bass-player said as they passed. From their grins it was impossible to tell if they had been fined by Mister Movin for their night's performance or given bonuses.

'Oh Robin,' the Press agent resumed, 'did I mention that approximately one-fourth Mister Movin's annual income is given back for scholarships and charities—?'

Captain Arthur led another boy down the ramp to the stage-door. He told him, 'I don't even want to hear what you got to say.'

The Press agent was white, bearded, obese, self-conscious, transparently untruthful, of doubtful efficiency and a companion of Mister Movin's boyhood.

'Robin, I know you waited eighteen hours—I *know*. You have to understand. This is no ordinary man—I know you understand. This man holds in his hands the faith of millions of people, Robin. Between shows, he has to—to regenerate. He knows you're here. He's seen you. Did you know he was watching you?'

'I,' continued the Preacher, 'am the master-at-arms and the chairman of the board. I am the master of my Fate and the Captain of my Soul. I am the man who make the Gospel Mash—'

He was not a minister: merely a disc-jockey named the Preacher.

'To you of the Lord I say, go ye out and do what Mister Movin says to do. That is'—here the Preacher deepened his voice to the sorrowful plumcake tone immortalized by Dr Martin Luther King. 'Get out and feel proud and walk tall and work hard, for the Colour of My Skin is a Glory not Sin!'

In the resounding of this, the Preacher looked hopefully towards the alcove.

'For he is great, he is pure, he is good, he is just, he

91

is hon'ble, he has it *all* together,' the Preacher said. 'He is of the Lord, surely a king among men and show business.'

Across the doorway to the auditorium, the arm of the guard stiffened, then dropped. The marshal up the steps came and through the crowd, checking the folds of his camel coat as if fearful of displacing teacups.

A girl followed. A girl with tiny shoulders and enormous Afro hair and a Mister Movin programme in both hands; looking about her through eyes with the enormous innocence of a child watching animals. She smothered the heart of the pilot of Mister Movin's private aircraft and filled each jolly deejay with hags' envy. For a moment she stood in the alcove, her hair outlined like a spread fan at the gleam of the dressing-room door.

The pilot was white, from Georgia and twenty-two years old. He lay at his ease on a pile of boxes, curtains and old flags.

'You know, Mist' Wielhaus,' he remarked to his companion, ' 'way I heard it, Mister Movin just keeps one whole attorney to deal with all the paternity suits that gets filed against him; you know if there's any truth in that, Mist' Wielhaus? ... All them ladies who tell the Judge Mister Movin was with them in Pensacola, Florida, the night he's playing in Baltimore, Maryland.'

'Robin,' said the Press agent, 'you have to understand the kind of man this is. His energy is unlimited. Why, he may have six different ones in six different motel-rooms, you know? He just calls for them as he wants them—'

The Press agent suddenly realized the Englishman was listening.

'But in *everything*,' the Press agent added hastily, 'he demands respect. Or, as Mister Movin puts it, *perceiving*. He puts 'em up on a pedestal. It's always formal. He never calls 'em anything but Miss Smith or Miss Jones—'

'Way I heard it,' the young pilot indiscreetly continued, 'Mist' Movin used to get his pick of the in-tire Miss Western World Pageant ever' year, just whichever those ladies he wanted. But he never wanted none of 'em. You know if there's any truth in that, Mist' Wielhaus?'

'I do not,' replied his companion. 'All I know is, that durned Go-Go dancer wants *my* tail and she was durned near after it on the flight in from Washington.'

'Right there on the *airplane*?' the pilot said, impressed.

He looked with wonder, and the other man with foreboding, at the rear prospect of the dancer, still engaged with the Preacher in conversation of a philosophical nature. Between her tall, white boots and the bearskin of her wig, there seemed no body whatever: only a bone-hipped bottom that jutted so that a glass might balance on it.

The unwilling object of her scheduled-flight attentions was little and whiter than white, with toothbrush hair and clothes like a Grand Canyon tourist. No boyhood friend of Mister Movin, he was, nevertheless, one person among the anxious crowd of boyhood friends who might expect to be beckoned through the alcove by the marshal at any time. He was a sound-engineer: the one in the world who could contain Mister Movin in a recording-studio. He collected chess-sets and preferred to be in bed by midnight.

'And he ain't goin' to buy the '73 Cadillac Bro'ham 'cause it's too small for Mrs Movin to squeeze inside of, you know if that's true at all, Mist' Wielhaus?'

'Maybe,' the engineer said.

From a low stool, a man with a pipe in his mouth spoke up. He looked like a doctor; more so than the real doctor did. He was the comedian in the show, Coon Ass.

93

'Hey,' Coon Ass said, ' 'member when he done put her on a diet?'

'A *diet*,' the pilot exclaimed.

'Sho's Hell a diet,' Coon Ass agreed. 'Sent her into reducin' parlours—she wasn't goin' to eat no peach pie, no chilli, Mumbo sauce, muffins—uh-*uh*. I tell you, man, she was gonna be so *skinny*...'

Up the steps from the auditorium, Mr La Rosa now appeared, striking himself with a newspaper in an angry manner, and there was a small revival backstage. Even fallen from power, by remaining invisible for long periods between shows, Mr La Rosa continued to possess a star's reflected importance.

'So tell us what *happened*!' the pilot said.

'He was in Washington,' said Coon Ass, 'playin' Loew's Palace, stayin' at the Sonesta. He had done four shows that night. It's late. He goes back to the hotel, and finds her with—a whole *box* of Hershey bars in her room!'

Coon Ass laughed: the tricky, thin, black *heh-heh-heh* which he was so uncertain of ever drawing from his audiences.

'Wow-ee!' he added, 'she's so spreadable, it's in-*credible*!'

His laughter died out.

All of them looked dreadfully towards the alcove.

Coon Ass swallowed; he found his neck missing.

But it was only Mr Pegley who came out, smoking a nice cigar.

'Oh-kay—' began Mr La Rosa furiously, but there was no need to list penalties. From the underground dressing-rooms, people had already started to appear too early—bandsmen and Mister Movin's chorus the Lamp-Liters and the two Go-Go dancers who during the show pumped their limbs in long shadows from a dais above his head.

The Englishman awoke in the deepest misery. Seeing

his notebook, a theatre guard inquired, 'You writin' a song?'

Mister Movin's supporting players stood together.

The Lamp-Liters, from the back of the theatre, were boys in pink dungarees like brazen girls.

From the side of the theatre, at close quarters, they were heavy-faced men of thirty who seldom smiled; whose fuzzy polls had been unhappily rinsed in ginger to hide the sparks of grey.

Coon Ass got up from the stool, knocking out his pipe. He was paralysed down one side.

The second Go-Go girl was white—horribly scarred at the ribs by the attempts of whalebone to give her a shape. Onstage, no one would spare her a glance, or her larger shadow. But the black girl without a body, only boots—surely she would take a shiver from Mister Movin's audience as she danced above him; in the raise of her knees, as she rotated the exquisite bunch of her ass, as she revealed again, under the tall wig, her lovely, tiny, contemptuous face.

Backstage, she turned.

She had a harelip.

Dwarfs make a superstar.

Honey went to the control-board. The creeping cold, in the wings of the theatre and beyond, grew once more radiant with expectation.

All doors stand open to the foyer. The waiting darkness is cool, for all that no movement is possible in it of any kind: the aisles are full and the sides of the pillars, the seats have been full for ever. Nothing dares stir but the face of a guitar on the stage and its reflection, wallowing high on the wall of the auditorium like wave-shadows against a boat.

Coon Ass tells frightful jokes. From the trim little pipe-smoker backstage, his only hope is transformation

to a staring imbecile in a plantation-hat, who thumps
the boards with a stick and cymbal, croaking:

'*We shall overco-ome.*'

'Get outa here!'

'You don't do no Rock and Roll.'

'*—'long as we kin ru-un!*'

But, crash! They laugh. It's two o'clock. They snuggle
in their seats; take a last rest. Hold their breath or
giggle with almost terrified anticipation in the darkness
encircling the faintly green stage but the gun has gone
Mister Movin didn't come on like a normal man he's
on started here already clipping the microphone from
its stand he's here he's started he's here even in that
commonplace gesture fully launched on the constant
staircase of his own feet he's *here.*

It's over. Eight songs. Eight was it? One song. Spun in
hot whips that lay the sweat in an ace of spades across
his back as he turns to the band, not to let them take a
bow, not to compliment them but urge them, his trouser-
legs rippling like rags—further—two fists in a walking-
race—further, further, watch me, I've got it, watch me
now, me, until his voice has gone and the screams, the
flashing swans of brass, all gone into what cannot be
broken: a tom-tom, but—*no*—someone comes from the
wings on ordinary legs, *no*, leads him away and he goes,
no, no, he's going, *no*, they're taking him, *no no, God*

A drum snaps and a hard white light

He throws the cloak—

Exact with the drum, precise to the light

—*Aside.*

Yes, back without walking, *yes*, back by that rapid
staircase, *yes*, back to open arms of sound from people
who know that after all, *yes*, it is only just beginning...

The curved drawbridge of the Hotel Majesta becomes
an overpass by which one may gain access to the freeway,

the horizon and beyond, the next Hotel Majesta. That, too, standing elegant as a salted cracker, offers, among its awnings, the same tropic-gardens and motor-lodges, the same warm-water pool, airline offices, bank, florist, Executive Health Club and Sauna and Pink Moose Calico Coffee Shop; the same kind of hamburger-pickle and, above all, the same infallible access to the freeway to the next Hotel Majesta.

You may depend in particular upon Majesta lobbies, upon their dull gold furnishings and immobilized lamps, but this snowy afternoon, in a certain Majesta lobby there is a serious flaw. It is occupied by groups of black men; its trustworthy brocades disturbed by the chiffon and orange and butcher-boy stripes which the black men wear as they sport or recline insolently around one perfectly appalled old lady put to wait, as old ladies so often are, right in the middle.

She grips a purse with a gilt attachment to hold her gloves. Under their elastic, her legs appear bandaged. She is recently widowed, she has only half a stomach, another beef-black matador prances by and, oh! it is too much.

'Sonny, will you come here, please?'

The doorman, whose ears protrude beneath his scarlet top hat, is uncommonly young. He accepts from the old lady a lemon-flavoured cough-drop.

'My Harry—' she tells him, 'died in spite of the Hand that guided from above. So I am learning to practise SAM, Sorrowing thru' Adjustment to Maturity.'

The old lady raises her voice for the benefit of the group nearest to her on the sofas; their eyes sightless behind violet-tinted shades, the pink gum snapping against their teeth.

'Sonny, how old are you? Nineteen? Well, you're a fine man. Hair cut short like a man. Stay a man, that's all I say to you—*stay* a man.'

97

Snow and wet blow into the lobby and out again with the revolving door; which delivers, huddled in a preposterous short fur-coat, the Press agent and then the little audio-engineer who collects chess-sets. After they have spoken on the house-phone, however, it is the engineer by himself who approaches the panel of onyx elevators. His companion sits heavily down on a chaise-longue before a Versailles-type mirror where an Englishman is awakening from an unhappy doze.

'Hi, how's it going?' calls out some rollicksome black. The old lady seems about to faint.

'—Sonny, will you come here a moment, please?'

'Robin, you're not mad with me. Robin, you have to realize, you have to understand—I know this man upstairs, we were kids together, he and I. Here you're dealing with the faith, with the dreams of thirty million people. Understand? He needs time. He knows you're here. He's a little leery of you. He's been asking about you—'

The engineer left the elevator at 'Alaska Suite', stepping into a carpet like a white poodle's back. Farther down the white hall, a camel overcoat straightened up, a dark, dangerous scar of eyes regarded him, then the marshal sat back again out of sight. As a further precaution, the suite's white double-doors were blocked by a despoiled room-service trolley. After knocking and answering a challenge, the engineer had to insinuate himself around the edge of it, taking care for his cuffs in salad dressing and melted ice.

In a fussy white drawing-room full of iron patio furniture, a fat woman vacuumed the carpet. The man who had admitted the engineer returned to a studio couch and resumed looking down through the folds of his robe at the pouch between his skinny black legs. He was eating an orange. The suite smelled sharp with it. Orange peel curled from every visible ash-tray.

The man was—an accountant? Mister Movin's financial advisor. Spread next to him on the couch were papers which the engineer recognized as box-office returns, achieved or anticipated, on the present concert-tour from the Boston Garden to the Harlem Apollo. Assuredly it was Nature's duty to confer some keenness of intellect upon the man, for he was small and ugly as hate with a primitive jaw, hair rising to a comic piccaninny point and a voice full of splinters and old bottles. Absorbed as he was in the logistics of Mister Movin's tour, the contents of his underpants seemed to fascinate him more. Still looking down into the pouch, he remarked:

'Mister Movin done forty-eight thousand dollars in three nights.'

The engineer had to talk about recording-time booked for Mister Movin in this city between shows. The man on the couch, staring into his pouch, demanded, 'They gonna pay Mister Movin his money at the studio?'

At the engineer's reply, he scowled more intensely downwards and spat orange pips into his shut fist.

'—They say it's kinda hard to get that kinda money drawn on a weekend. They'll have their cheque made out.'

In a voice roughened to near-incomprehensibility, the man on the couch said, 'Mister Movin don't goin' to take no cheque. You tell those cats Mister Movin don't ree-cord noplace without he get paid *at* the studio. How else you think Mister Movin don't get cheated, huh? He don't want to be blunt with you, Mist' Wielhaus, but you got to inform them cats at Monarch Records that they got pay Mister Movin right there in the studio, same as always or Mister Movin don't ree-cord *nothin*'!'

The engineer had anticipated this response.

'Mr La Rosa at the theatre?'

99

'Yeah,' the engineer said. 'He asked if Mister Movin wants to work out with the band tomorrow?'

'Tonight,' the man on the couch said. 'After the show.'

After the *third* show. After three nights of three shows, each one of which by itself might have torn the city down, Mister Movin had been known to rehearse his musicians a twelve hours further so young horn-players swooned away. And still that same night, on a fresh stage, in some other desperate place he would be miraculously re-created.

'Mr Gelman's right here in the lobby.'

The man on the couch showed his teeth at this reference to Mister Movin's boyhood companion, the Press agent.

'He asked me to say to Mister Movin there's a reporter that's been waiting. From England.'

The man spat more pips into his fist.

'Mister Movin don't goin' speak to no ree-porter and you know why, Mist' Wielhaus? 'Cause Mister Movin already superhip to these guys. He can tell 'em what they goin' to ask 'fore they even ask it.'

The fat woman came back into the drawing-room carrying one of the Hotel Majesta's stately waste-paper tins which she placed between the man's legs as if in reproof for the orange-peel he was letting fall. He himself now talked into the telephone. His little finger scratched the crimson tail of his eye in a gesture of surprising effeteness, compared to the black weight of his jaw.

'You reahlly need those promo's?' he demanded.

'I need 'em,' said the voice in the receiver.

'You got a tape-machine there?'

'Yeah, I got one.'

Suddenly the man flung himself backwards on the couch with legs wide apart, scratching his pouch while his eyes searched the gold-leaved ceiling for inspiration.

Then, as the tape ran at the other end of the telephone, he declaimed:

'Hi ever'body, this is Mister Movin.'

He reflected.

'I think the People,' he intoned, 'is beginnin' to understand. We not here to tear it down—we here to talk it *up*!'

On the floor beside him were some of the two hundred pairs of shoes he wore out each year onstage—patent and piebald and pigskin in a triple row like a harbour of picturesque craft.

'Now li'l brother and li'l sister,' Mister Movin recited, 'if you on your way to school—and you feelin' bad. Remember—a education can give you what you never had. So don't feel bad, just say it agin—'

And he spoke an axiom which, though not clever in the least, had struck alert the soul of a nation.

'The Colour of My Skin is a Glory not Sin.'

In the next few minutes Mister Movin extemporized five or six more promotional flashes for programmes on the Soul radio stations he owned. The engineer rose but was signalled to wait. The fat woman brought a second wastepaper tin. Tenderly she raised Mister Movin's feet from their slippers and placed one in each of the tins, which were filled with warm water and salts.

'—and fire Jack O'Diamond,' Mister Movin said, 'over his ratings. Yeah.' He hung up. The fat woman pushed back the coffee table. Kneeling, she laid one of Mister Movin's feet into the vastness of her apron and began to rub ointment into it.

The engineer watched. He simply did his job. All he desired was to be approved of as a technician and to get to bed, unhampered by a Go-Go dancer, before midnight. He seemed to be the only creature living who had not enjoyed the friendship of Mister Movin's boyhood; yet the star's good opinion had descended radiantly on him to his complete mystification. Try as he might, the engineer could only attribute this to a chance remark of his concerning Cincinnati, Ohio; after which Mister Movin, hugging him briefly, had exclaimed with the warmest hoarseness, 'You reahlly dig those German folks, don't you, Mister Wielhaus?' So he received Mister Movin's deepest confidences. He lip-read where it was possible.

The fat woman now sat on the couch. In the shelter of her, Mister Movin remarked, 'This is where she gets to work on *me*.'

She took one of his hands under her arm. She spread the fingers on her great, beige front to trim the cuticles; and, innocently dwarfed by her, Mister Movin suddenly released the most blissful smile. 'People sure like Mister Movin when Esther's on the road with him, don't they, honey?

' 'F I'm on the road alone,' he continued, 'I just like a teenager, nineteen, twenty years old, bam, bam, bam, 'cause that racehorse—he don't run, Mist' Wielhaus, if he ain't got no lust, right? I'll eat a hamburger 'fore a show that I don't even finish, but with her along—today I ate almost a full meal with salad and Black Forest dessert.

'We could hire a maid to do all this, Mist' Wielhaus, only she don't want it. She's the one has to salt my feet and rub my back and give me my heart-pill and take the ingrowin' hairs outa my nose that I'd hurt myself if I tried.'

Mister Movin leaned forward—his wife corrected his position with a little tug of the arm.

'Now you may think she looks kinda a large size, but she gives me a lotta' room in the bed. I don't do any karate tricks, you understand, but I have to spread me out a lot.'

'You ever dream?' asked the engineer.

Himself, he dreamed occasionally of an English ivory chess-set.

Mister Movin thrust out his jaw as he did to an innocent remark which he suspected of containing anarchy or plagiarism. Then he relaxed. His wife began his other hand.

'Ninety-five per cent pleasant dreams,' he replied. 'If I eat late, I'll dream of a accident, and that's not pleasant. But then I wake and see the shape o' her in the bed and I feel like I did sleepin' at the back of the aunt I boarded with when I was twelve years old.'

Mister Movin stared up at his wife.

'She brings me a soda. I drink a little of it. If she's with me, Mist' Wielhaus, it feels like my spirit and all the wild things goes out of me and lies in peace on the couch in the next room 'till morning.'

... How can he stop when, by six false endings, six different coloured cloaks coddling his head like a child from the bath and thrown off exact with the drum, he tells them it is everlasting? How can he break the grip of the spirits that whirl him, themselves in the grip of a tom-tom?

How can they release him to any other city? He belongs only here, is perfect for this stage alone. The hair lapping his ears like an exquisite cloth of berries—smoke of his skin against a leotard—the shining cables of his chest and arms—the butt of the captive between his legs, that makes women scream, men say 'Yeah' and the tom-tom obey—he is theirs, and will they not shed blood to keep him.

He has slowed it to the chip of the guitar, the eight beats and eight of the bass, the bumps of the celebration in the aisles below him, the high knee-shadows of unregarded Go-Go dancers rising behind—slow, *I got it, watch me*, he smiles, his eyes are closed, the captive strains at his crotch, he needs nothing, nobody, the smile is 'I', a huge plate of conceit but it touches the people smaller than himself, transformed to the pride they should justly feel but have been denied; *watch me, watch me, now*.

The curtains start to move, *no*, he repeats in a dust-storm whisper, one phrase—*no, no*, the curtains advance and with them a police captain, two guards and a man in a camel overcoat, jabbing pettishly with fingers at such shapes as propose to climb the stage, *stay, watch me now, no stay*, the same phrase he repeats, *Soul heart, Soul Heart, Soul Heart*, in a city where little is judged to be satisfactory entertainment that does not end in tears, *Soul Heart*, where the very peace has a quality of angry breathing, *Soul Heart, Soul Heart*—the audience turns and dances into the street.

Beany

'Her glandular trouble seems to have flared up again, poor Beany,' Mrs McIsaac said. 'One tick—I'll plug the phone extension by her bed.' Benita's voice came on, at once establishing that Ian had to ask what was wrong. She kept telling him 'Oh *I'm* all right, go and do your music'; but each word, each long pause was filled with the concrete of reproach.

Half-an-hour later, he was on his way to see her. It felt strange, like school turned round for examinations, because normally Ian went to Denison Grange only at weekends. Then, as he turned into the farm-road, his brain rang a sudden peal of approaching holidays. No more Sunday drinks, he thought. No more Clock Golf. No more Saturdays claimed by significant attendance at weddings of friends of hers.

Before marriage to Captain McIsaac, Benita's mother had been, among varied and enterprising things, a trained nurse. At the kitchen-garden door she intercepted Ian, a lioness shielding her cub, even though it was the force of her hints rather than Benita's which brought him out all this way. She looked fiercely at him; that there should be no mistaking the source of the glandular trouble. 'Now you're not to be too long if Beany's not well.' And once he had imagined Mrs McIsaac herself rather desired him.

Benita occupied a very large room at the top of the main staircase, overlooking the paddock. She sat in her four-poster bed with a shawl round her, a pink knitted shawl, and her blonde hair was newly washed and set. A lifelong care not to disturb it as she moved had bowed her shoulders somewhat.

'I'm so fed up,' she said at once.

'What on earth for?'

Her skis curved from the top of the linen press. An ornate fireplace had been blocked in by a white radiator, the surface of which was covered by small animals of china, porcelain and pottery.

'Don't you like working at the Conservative Offices?'

She burst into tears. '*Yes*—just being a goody-goody little secretary at the Conservative Offices!' An extra crump of angry skin appeared, somehow, in Benita's neck as she wept, and licks of clean hair swung over both cheeks. Ian looked away. His abstracted gaze met his own face a dozen times—beside a horse, a van, a gate, with his guitar demonstrating a tricky chord. On every possible surface in the room there stood a photograph of him.

'Look, are you angry with me?'

'No,' Benita answered; a patrician and indistinct 'Ne-aw'.

'I *know* I'm going to London. If this bloke Robin's going to take me on, I've just got to—'

'Oh, don't *shout* at me,' she whispered.

'It's a London band.'

'I know it's a London band,' she wept.

She could not hear the singing in the words. And Ian, notwithstanding his terror that Mrs McIsaac might come up, found it increasingly difficult to concentrate. Benita was really miserable; her desolation emphasized by some surgical-smelling ointment. But nowadays his future was so close to him, and sometimes caught

his throat so hard, he could pity *anyone* who wasn't
him.

'It's *us*.'

Benita had mentioned this partnership before; from
other sickbeds, so it always put Ian in mind of a warm
drink.

'You never—'

'Never what?' he demanded irritably.

'Oh, nothing!'

Finally Benita made him induce her to add, 'You
never tell me anything; you never—*say* anything.' She
seemed to gain a little in confidence. 'They all keep
going on at me.'

'Who, your mother?'

'Mummy—the Captain—Miss Mannish. Oh you
know!' she exclaimed, flushed and passionate and dis-
infected. ' "When's Ian going to"—oh, you know!
"When's Ian going to *do* something?" '

The matter was not eased by Benita's reluctance to
speak the name of the thing he might or might not 'do';
and, in his own avoidance of it, Ian found himself de-
barred from all expressions of comfort excepting a vague
goodwill. Nor would Mrs McIsaac say it, although later,
outside the bedroom holding a mug of tea for Benita,
she almost came to the point.

'Beany spent *months* knitting you that pully.'

He had worn it tonight hoping it might assist the
glandular trouble to abate. It was, indeed, lovingly
cable-stitched, but too tight.

'*And* she made you that table-lamp out of the Grappa
bottle from her holiday.'

'You've all been really good to me here: I can't thank
you enough.'

'Yes,' Mrs McIsaac agreed. 'Otherwise you'd have
been just sitting over in those digs. We took you
up. You were in all of our plays. And, you know, you

have monopolized Beany—getting her to drink her tea over the phone and saying you loved the sound of her swallowing—'

At this spectre of infatuation, Ian blushed violently.

'You say it's money,' Mrs McIsaac continued. 'I always thought Pop what-do-you-call-its made tons of money.'

'But I haven't got a contract yet.'

'Mm.' She frowned. 'And you know, even the Captain's starting to ask me "Who *is* this fellow Ian and what does he think he's up to?"'

'And Beany's got *such* a nice job at the Conservative offices, she ought to be *so* cheerful. We got her those beautiful golf-clubs. There's no need for all this glandular business. The Captain said he could make both of you a really nice flat over the Coach House. The Captain's awfully well-off, you know: if you could just—'

At last it came out; what he, with *his* future, ought to 'do'.

'—just get engaged. Just engaged. It would make *such* a difference to Beany at the moment.'

Benita and her mother came through the stable-yard wearing car-coats of chocolate-coloured suede, scarves pushed back from the hair, knotted at the cleft of the chin, and sensible shoes. Two yellow Labradors foraged, tails-up, about the large stones marking the curve of the farm road—they were mother and daughter, too, and somewhat easier to tell apart from a distance.

Mrs McIsaac said, 'Oh, I *do* hope Rebecca isn't going to find a rats' nest in the paddock.'

'Bec-ca!' Benita called in a harsh baritone. Her mother contributed a noise like the whoop of a tug which had also been known to attract the dogs.

'Only darling, for God's sake keep dry and warm— I've nursed you all these weeks.'

'Just my bunnies are cold.'

But Mrs McIsaac, despite this limiting of the cold to Benita's hands, began to tremble with an anxiety which came if her simplest arrangement was put to the test. They managed the paddock-gate however, and the tractor-ruts. They stood in the field with backs cushioned by the wind, their collar-fur whipping and flicking as the dogs moved about far away.

'Mummy, you're not going to invite the Ffords, are you!'

'Sweetheart, we must. They've been saying to us all summer, "Oh you must come over and swim and play tennis", and Daddy Fford's really awfully sweet.'

'His breath smells of Big-Jobs,' Benita complained.

'Oh,' her mother gasped, 'Beany! Your feet are soaking. Oh, and Becca's found a rats' nest; I can't bear those naked pink tails! Oh, I shall go mad.' It was these diverse strains upon the arrangement of the walk that caused Mrs McIsaac to turn into the wind again, to a subject Benita dreaded.

'Now,' she said, 'Beany, is Ian coming to our dance or isn't he? Because obviously I've got to know the exact numbers of young people to leave cold food for in the schoolroom.'

At Mrs McIsaac's New Year's dance, young and old were divided. Benita's friends remained at Denison Grange and had cold ham. Their elders undertook a complex formal dinner of which each course was eaten at a different house in the neighbourhood, returning later for coffee, liqueurs and the Conga.

Scarlet to the knot of her headscarf, Benita answered that she didn't know.

'What does that mean? "I don't know." '

'Mummy, I haven't heard from Ian yet.'

'Doesn't he write to you?'

Mrs McIsaac was angered by the thought of the letters

which daily left the Grange, addressed 'C/o Flaming Ember Productions' in Benita's large, loyal radiant-blue handwriting. Then, like a bat, her mood flew another way. 'I just know there won't be enough Gin and French for all of them—that Sally Fford drinks like an absolute fish.'

They were standing beside a tree that had blown down in the paddock, dragging wicked blue clay up with its gashed roots—this was when the awful thing happened. Benita never took the dogs near the tree again.

'You know, darling, last summer—before that young man started mucking around and having to play that ukelele of his every second—'

Benita, in a small voice, said, 'It's a guitar.'

'Sweetheart, I used to watch the two of you walking beside the Motte with your arms wrapped round one another, and think to myself "Oh, they're going to have *such* lovely children". I believe it's going to snow; and there'll be horrid black ice. Beany darling, you must *know* what he's up to in London. He told me it was money, but surely he must be earning decent money— he's on television enough.'

Benita knew. She dared not watch television.

'Well, darling,' her mother said jovially, 'what *is* this fellow up to?'

'*I* don't know, Mummy.'

Benita started to cry.

'He's been gone four months.'

'I *know* he has.'

'What's he *doing*?'

'It's a London band.'

'Tch, even that dreadful Bella Walmisley with her great big enormous nose has got herself engaged now; and they say her leg will never be right again after Verbier. You see, darling, you have to start thinking about getting everything ready so far in advance, if you want a really sweet little church and a Tudor barn for the reception and—'

Was it a desperate wish that her mother should not be denied these arrangements that made Benita, next to the fallen tree, tell her, 'Well—we're probably going to announce it.'

'Your engagement!' Then her mother cut herself off. 'No.'

'Yes'—for by saying, it became wonderful, if not yet official.

Mrs McIsaac grew defensive.

'Well, that's a nice way for a young fellow to behave, I don't think; not a word to anyone about it. Well, he can jolly well speak to me about it first, *and* to the Captain, because darling, don't forget who paid for you to go to Benenden and to the Cordon Bleu.' But Mrs McIsaac realized that for her too, in the provisional guest-list, there now would be happiness and release.

'He can announce it at the dance—only you must make sure he waits until all of us oldies are back from our house-to-house dinner. *There,*' she said '—after all that fuss, and now I'm really looking forward to our party, aren't you, darling?'

They clung together beside the kitchen-garden door and rocked free of their outdoor boots. Mrs McIsaac added plaintively, 'And I *do* so love it when all the young people sit together in their evening dress on the stairs.'

'Yes,' Benita said.

For big occasions like the dance, the guests were sign-posted from a long way outside Denison Grange, down the farm road to the side of the house across a backwater of the lawns. Half-way up the path, behind each arrival a brisk *clock* sounded. This was the gate in the old wall shutting itself on a stout rubber-band mechanism devised for the purpose by the ingenious Captain McIsaac.

Clock said the gate. The Captain and Benita's mother had only just left for the house-to-house dinner. As usual, the first to arrive, much too early, was last summer's agricultural student. There was something the matter with the ribbed front of his evening-shirt. As much as he tucked it behind his cummerbund, it buckled forth again. As he followed Benita around, it protruded at the angle of a rather fat knight's breastplate.

This youth was one of the very few males over whom she had ever achieved a dominance, and she exercised it with the mercilessness of a precocious child. She made jokes about the noises he produced in the lavatory; informed him there was something wrong with his shirt; ordered him, on pain of having his hair ruffled, to help get the last things ready for the young people's supper in the schoolroom.

'How's Ian?' he ventured.

'Coming later,' Benita said quickly.

'He's made a disc now, hasn't he, or something?'

'You know very well he has.'

'I must get it actually. What does he call himself these days?'

'The Great Gatsby. It's a London band,' Benita answered in the bored voice that required all of her strength.

'Beany—'

'Oh, shut your bum fartface,' she said, praying for him to stop.

'Ian and you must have been together for about a year. I was just thinking,' the youth continued sentimentally, and tucked in his shirt, 'it must be getting close to your first anniversary.'

Clock. Next came the four daughters of the Rector of Staveley with Paxton Abbots—four, distinguished in track athletics and the pursuit of undergraduates.

Benita loathed them but they always came, and afterwards spread rumours about her. They stood in the small lobby, piling their coats into her arms, and all said 'Hell-eaw' on curious, high, flat, ecclesiastical notes. Two of them went straight into the drawing-room where the dancing would be, and started to interfere with her record-player. She had to stay in the hall and let in Hugh Forward who—*clock*—came next. He tittered.

Clock—and more young men of the district, scrum-halves and wags, filled the outer lobby, unwinding mufflers to display necks which their formal collars had turned to a brutal hunting-pink, and boastfully requesting sacks to protect their minimal sports-cars from the frost. Yet at first there was a great reluctance in all of them to move any further inside the house.

Among the cawing guests, Benita moved, showing below her long dress the point of one gilt shoe. She concealed the tremble of her heart in shrieking at the two dogs, who had escaped from Captain McIsaac's workshop to wreath the young men's evening-trousers in white hairs from their tails, Oh, and supposing he *did* come, but not in proper clothes! As Hugh Forward talked and tittered to her, Benita suddenly remembered the Christmas when her mother had threatened no presents for anyone unless Ian got his hair cut. *Oh stop saying 'Where's Ian?'* 'He's coming down later,' she answered. 'He's doing a recording.' From time to time she excused herself and ascended the main staircase. Below, one Rector's daughter nudged another, indicating the pain of the angle at which, for the sake of her hair, Benita carried her head.

Linda Gillies had a thrilling, low voice of which she made use on all occasions. She was Benita's best friend, and allowed to deposit her cloak on Benita's very own bed. Turning round from the collection of animals on top of the radiator she huskily said, 'You didn't have the little donkey and cart, Beany, when I last saw these.'

'You can stay the night can't you, Loopy, and make a weekend of it?'

Linda nodded vigorously.

'But Mummy says this time you're not to follow the Captain round in the morning, pushing him and saying, "When are you going to get two bathrooms?"'

Both cackled. Then—she couldn't help it—Benita held up her left hand with its little finger crooked as if to allow room on the second finger for a ... Linda understood. She went owl-eyed, gathering the thrill into her throat. Before she could make a sound, the telephone rang. The extension was already plugged next to Benita's bed, menaced on all sides by framed photographs of Ian.

Benita answered it. The party sent an enticing strump through the floor. Twirling in her turquoise before the wardrobe mirror, Linda was thinking of the wedding and such further weddings as would be grouped around it; of receptions in thirteenth-century barns, the log fires with young men perspiring above them, and every other thing which so wonderfully concludes romance; the people one meets.

'I'm afraid Ian's going to be rather late,' Benita told her. 'He's still at the recording-studio—he says he's just leaving.'

Linda caught her arm.

'But you will announce it tonight!'

'Yes.'

'When? At midnight?'

'Yes,' said Benita.

'Oh su-uper!'

She did notice that Benita turned away from the phone scarlet to the pale roots of her hair. Whether this signified the Curse, a headache or the normal anxieties of supervising a cold buffet, Linda Gillies had no idea.

Arrival feels early; but, as they sat around the school-room with plates on their knees, it was already past ten o'clock. Supper passed almost in silence. A voice inquired, 'What are you doing now?' and was told, 'Working in a boutique.' Even the japester was rendered speechless through fear for his trousers on the dog-hairy sofas. Before serving the fruit-salad Benita took all the salad dishes out to the kitchen, piled them in the sink and squeezed soapy liquid over them.

The only real activity came from the Rector's daughters who, though fashioned of hurdles and good English beef, were considerably in demand. A succession of dancing-partners were strong-armed by them to the drawing-room: at last, when Benita had gone upstairs again, everyone followed and took up formalized raving-positions.

The young men stood with bodies straight and arms extended to push out several inches of shirt cuff. Their single movement in the dance was to replace occasionally the claw of hair that fell over their eyes; but out beyond every cuff, a girl in a long dress earnestly pirouetted.

'Oh, now where's Beany got to?' Linda Gillies demanded. She had obliterated her partner by sitting on his lap. As she bounced, only his turned-in evening pumps showed the agony it caused him.

Benita came back into the drawing-room.

'Is he here?' two or three voices asked.

'He's coming.'

'Ooo-er,' Linda called out. 'Is he bringing his band or anything?'

'Has he got a *dornse*-band?'

'It's a London band,' said Benita.

She stood with Hugh Forward in the shadow around

the gramophone that the Captain had built in only a matter of hours. Hugh held his wineglass against his shoulder and tittered. He had ceased to advance, either in physique or intelligence, when he was twenty—now he was forty-three. He was very sweet but a sore vexation to the arrangements of Mrs McIsaac, since he properly belonged in no age-group. Last year he had accompanied the grown-ups, eating each course of dinner at a different house. He was demoted this year, but didn't mind. He wore a bow tie somehow affixed to the collar of a tennis shirt.

A girl in velvet crossed the polished floor, leading her partner by the hand. Oh, and Mummy made such a fuss if the floor got scratched.

'Hullo Janet,' Hugh Forward said. He tittered.

'—Beany.'

'Yes.'

'When the others come back, we want to make an announcement.'

Her face froze.

'We want to announce our engagement,' the girl said, pretending to reel in her young man by the arm.

'Oh no, *please*!'

'Well, couldn't we make it a double-announcement?' the girl said.

'No *pleeease*!' Benita's shoulders ached with pleading, with climbing the stairs to listen for his van, with trying to keep her hair looking nice. Oh, the agonies and dead-weights and flushes of terror that surrounded the simple thing she wanted! Now she went from hot to cold at the commotion of dogs in the lobby; and Mrs McIsaac peeped conspiratorially round the door, like a jolly soul who would much rather be with the children.

'Oh!' she wailed. 'No one's *dancing*.'

Around her, the darkness moved with white shirt fronts and grown-up smells—garlic and the gymshoe

118

and rabbit's-cage of cigars relit after the car journey. A dozen perfectly formal voices spanning three generations said, 'Hell-eaw.'

'Come on!' Mrs McIsaac stepped down from her shoes. 'Who's going to do Strip the Willow!'

'Mummy, you're squiffy!'

'At Bunty McNish's we had the most beautiful Scampi Provençal, does our breath all stink of it, darling?'

She was in a very good mood. In stockinged feet she clasped her stole around her and laid her cheek romantically against it. 'Oh I *do* love to see all the young people—'

Laughter preceded Daddy Fford as if he was learning to throw his voice. 'Mhah mhah mhah,' he said. 'My little maid.'

'Hell-eaw,' said Benita.

'Mm, and where's your little box of tricks tonight, what's-his-name?'

'Ian. He's coming shortly.'

'Good, good,' said Daddy Fford looking straight past her.

'—and did you see,' a voice continued, 'all that stuff on television last night about the Poor? The *frytful* things they put in their stomachs!'

'Now look, darling!' Mrs McIsaac advanced, still without shoes but now in a temper. 'Is Ian coming or isn't he?'

'He is,' Benita whispered, 'he's on his way.'

'Because look, sweetheart—'

'My God! Where's old Captain got to? He's *not* gone back to building that damned boat of his!'

'Mhah hah hah.'

'Beany darling, it's not *good* enough. Making you wait for him like a—a—' Her mother giggled. 'Oh dear, the drinky brings all the truth out—like a wallflower. And I *did* so want you to meet a nice young Guards officer, and all you do is sit in the bath night after night, crying and biting your knees.'

'You *see*,' insisted the voice, 'that's the whole point. There's no need for them to eat the rubbish they do. Yes, and cods' balls. I mean, take the other night. I gave my three just a plain carrot salad. The Poor could manage that, surely to God: carrot—black pepper—oil—a pinch of tarragon—'

'I'm *not*,' wept Benita. A Beatles record had come on; dreadful, hateful, horrible. Nearby, Daddy Fford was saying, 'Well, ay make no secret of the fact that *ay*—don't like 'em at all, not one little bit, beggin' your pardon, Ma'am.' In the twilight, the Mister Punch impression in his carved cheeks was reinforced by the modest size of his legs.

'Ay mean,' continued Daddy Fford, 'the guitar, played in the proper way, is a beautiful instrument, yes? But not the way these types—what? Nasty little things. Nasty little things.'

'Help in a-ny way,' sang the Beatles.

'Na-sty lit-tle things,' sang Daddy Fford.

'Sweetie,' Daddy Fford said, abruptly intense. 'Sweetie—dance with an old man.'

'But Daddy, you're not to get saucy.'

'All or nothing at all, what? Mhah-hah!'

He and Mrs McIsaac moved off with necks arched like swans.

'Will you dance, Beany?'

It was Roger Lusada; five foot-three.

Benita saw her mother strike Daddy Fford jovially on the hand, then, still in her stockinged feet, Mrs McIsaac went round the darkened edges of the room, appealing to one after another group of young guests, as if Benita could not really be trusted to have looked after them. 'Now for God's sake, tell me the truth. Was there enough to eat in the schoolroom?'

'Yes heaps—honestly.'

'You're old enough to call me Dulcie, you know,' Mrs McIsaac told them reproachfully. At another point Benita heard her say, 'It's so sick-making, isn't it, the way some people carry on?'

'This one has got awfully good rhythm, hasn't it?' Roger Lusada volunteered.

'—almost midnight, we're all here,' Mrs McIsaac said to another group. 'We specially hurried through our pudding at the Dressers'. And all that champagne's sitting out in the deep freeze. It's so sick-making when people don't bother to turn up on time.'

Then her attention cut off another way as, after dinner, a grown-up person's will.

'I warn you,' Mrs McIsaac said, 'if anyone can play the piano, I shall simply throw myself at his feet.'

Somebody came through from the winter-garden.

He said, 'Beany—ahm, I'm afraid Linda's been a bit sick into the geranium.'

And Benita, who had discovered the very best parties are those one is not quite old enough to stay up for, replied in a flat voice, 'It's all right, it's dead anyway.'

Fun House

All the blinds were drawn on the second floor. From the doorstep the girls looked up and this reassured them. Wasn't darkness in daylight always part of having fun? Every day the girls clutched the house and searched the windows until their eyes hurt. Even in the rain, from within it thrilled to them yet like a wasp in a box— fun.

But the house was now mainly unoccupied. Its three owners, despite the aching of the girls, seldom called there. The coming of their business-manager, Mr Fonzei, had terminated fun in the most appalling way: with the sack. Already, Music Publishing had been expelled; and Graphics, which used to improve, for fun, the white walls of Nash terraces; even the sacred enclave attempting to market, for fun, a small radio inside an orange. Unemployment was never part of having fun.

Fine people some of these casualties had been, with soft voices, with trousers sprayed various colours, and yet savaged by Mr Fonzei, irrespective of trousers. Others might expect to be flung out tonight after a meeting upstairs this afternoon—nor were meetings ever part of having fun. Even the tea lady had been sacked, for all that she was among the very few professionals ever to have worked there.

Fun, among other things, encourages tramps. The Irishman who had come to the Press Office to ask for money to buy two hundred dolls to burn with napalm in the King's Road as a protest against war. Rodney gently said no. But the Irishman remained poignantly unaware of the idiocy of his plan: that both napalm and the King's Road had grown equally unfashionable.

'Hey, Rodney!' he exclaimed. 'How do you like my overcoat? Can you guess where I got it though? In a dustbin in Oxford Street!'

'And do you realize,' Rodney said, 'The Bat will spend two hundred pounds to have his clothes made like that?'

All of them still queued to talk to Rodney; the tramps, the plunderers, the soft voices. So long as Rodney was there in different shirts each day, answering the phone 'Hel-lo' on his indulgent double-note, those rich old times of twelve months ago could not utterly have vanished. Could they?

At that moment the Press Office loudspeakers released the first song of an album. It was the newest to have come from the three owners of the house; the myth from which Rodney himself was inseparable. On the doorstep the girls heard it, so did a surgical ward in a hospital three streets away. For a while the power and beauty and humour of its songs filled the house. And filled the house, too, with the happy illusion that the three parts of that myth were still one, in fun. Out in the rain, the girls dreamed of the night when it was recorded. To be fun it had to have been all night: all night and laughing.

'The Bat used to come in every morning at nine sharp, do his tracks and go home by Tube,' Rodney said. 'We had to ring Stevie up a lot in Scotland—little Hazel there did. Stevie finally posted us a few tapes he'd happened to drum, and some of those fitted, luckily.'

The journalist said, 'How about Shane?'

'Oh yes, Shane co-operated.'

'But Rodney, you sued him!'

'No, we issued a writ—Fonzei issued a writ. That signifies nothing at all; anybody can issue a writ. Shane issued a writ back. I didn't come into the office for a week, there were so many writs flying round.'

Writs were never part of having fun.

On the album, the third voice joined the other two. The girls on the street heard it and their bodies wept to touch his face, only touch, as the voice rose and fell like an angel.

'We got Shane to come along,' Rodney said, 'in the end. Did he say anything to either of the other two? He had a word with Stevie on the phone.'

'Well, it was always Stevie and Shane together. In the music.'

'Yes. Ah well ... He rang up Stevie and said, "I've gotta record this album. But I'll get you. *And* your fuckin' baby."'

The blinds being drawn, few of the amusing objects with which the Press Office had been furnished, for fun, were more than perplexing outlines; a rubber-plant or a tailor's dummy. By the door stood a developing-tray with toy birds around it, dipping their beaks in perpetual motion. The only illumination was the beam of a projector on Rodney's secretary's desk, that threw colours, wriggling, travelling, across one wall. Each new arrival crossed the beam, casting a giant blacksmith shadow on the wall as he advanced to shake hands with Rodney; that mark of any nation of idlers.

The Press Office was full—the system of luxurious couches that stretched from the nodding birds by the door to Rodney himself in the shadows of the wall facing.

Because of the rain outside and the large concentration in the room of exactly the same kind of animal-skin coats there was a powerful odour, against the joss-sticks, of underground trains in wet weather.

The door opened. From every couch, startled topiary work arose, expecting to move round one more place towards Rodney. But it was only the remaining Press Office girl, Hazel.

'Delia's got in downstairs,' she announced.

Rodney drew his knees up into his chair. This, irrespective of fun, was a beautiful object; a great peacock spray of basketwork. 'Delia!' he repeated. 'My God, Delia!' One deep shirt-cuff pushed the hair off his eyes and back it fell in place again, neat as the rim of a weir. His age was impossible to guess.

'Delia,' Rodney explained, 'belonged to Stevie. Part of the time she belonged to Stevie. When Stevie got married, Delia came to me and said, "If you won't tell me where Stevie's hiding, at least give me some money for my teeth."'

'She's fallen in the area trying to get in the studio window,' Hazel added. 'Her head's cut open.'

A telephone went 'peep'. Even the phones had once been fun.

'Hel-lo,' Rodney said. He pushed hair off his eyes: it fell back. 'Hel-lo, Audrey dear. Audrey, I can give you nothing yet on the meeting—'

A scuffle from overhead corroborated that the meeting was still in session.

'That's it, call in. We're on our way home, Audrey,' Rodney said as if calming a pony. 'That'll be very nice: have a drink and hear the new album. They're like they were at the very beginning.'

And now, on the stereo, the very first album of all was playing; the one that had caused the sun to come up throbbing like a bass. In the Press Office, in the hearts of all its exciting young people, an agony ran through for the days when they were young.

'Delia,' Rodney said, 'has no teeth. A poor boy over there in an overcoat wants us to give him the money to burn dolls with napalm. None of them understand. The Bat would say "Oh hey, sure, man, here take it", but with Fonzei upstairs we can give no more money away. Of course, we're giving twenty-five per cent to Fonzei. What I mean is, we can give no more money away to the wrong people.'

'Doesn't a year of dreams always end with an accountant?' the journalist said.

'But Alan, if you're twenty years old, if you have nothing more to look forward to at twenty, for how long is it possible to have dreams? Millionaires don't have dreams, they have rumours. Shane—The Bat—Stevie—all this house ever was to any of them was a rumour. Doesn't a rumour always come back to you different from the thing you meant?'

The journalist—and the girls on the doorstep—could remember with what convulsions those dreams had tried to materialize. The dresses from doomed boutiques given away at the ground-floor windows; the ten thousand balloons released from the roof for some purpose or other. Fun, after all, is the by-product of something else which has not quite succeeded.

Rodney murmured again, 'With Fonzei, we can give no more money away to the wrong people.'

'Who are the wrong people?' the journalist inquired.

From his chair Rodney looked out at the many beautiful silhouettes around him.

'The deaf,' he answered. 'And the blind.'

There is, between playing one album and the next, a short but desperate vigil. The scuffles seemed to increase from the boardroom over their heads. Rodney leaned from the corner of his chair to the journalist and said almost in a whisper, 'Oh they *need* you to write about them, Alan, they *need* it; they have so few friends left. But you see, Alan, they wear no watches.'

'Aren't any of them coming in for this meeting?'

'No. If you offer them a sweet now they say "give it to Fonzei". Fonzei is their big sponge. Fonzei's the one to go into the pantry and clean up the dog's mess.'

Many journalists rested beside Rodney in the afternoons, drowsing away their edition-times in a black fur of Scotch and Coke that covered their brains. There were the fat, disgusting old teen-page writers from national daily papers whose expressions remained fixed, as they drank, on the collar-stud bottoms of girls arriving and departing. To these, and even to the shabby Italian suits of the music trade press, Rodney's great gift was his full attention.

This journalist was different, however, or fondly imagined that he was. He declined all refreshment. He had an exceptional memory, with which he was breaking an unwritten rule of gratitude and love that Rodney himself, in stories about the house and its owners, should never directly be quoted. He had been commissioned by an American magazine. His brief (he had not mentioned) was to write, if the magazine should endure long enough to publish it, an obituary: for the house, its owners, the business-managership of Mr Fonzei and all the years of fun. Then, New York need no longer feel envious of anything.

'—but I mean, do you think I should get Schwartzmann to come in this afternoon?' the journalist pleaded. Schartzmann was the photographer. For each day of his attendance Schwartzmann was paid what the journalist received per month.

Rodney answered in the corralling tone of voice by which he always pronounced general unavailability.

'Shane hasn't been near the place for months, as you know. You *know* the position there, Alan. Nor Stevie. The Bat may come in later.'

'Any idea what time, though?'

Rodney smiled tolerantly.

'The Bat's got to come in sometime about his American trip, and we ma-ay be able to slip you in there for a few moments, but you have to do it so-o subtly, Alan, just sli-ide people under their noses. They shake no hands; they have no memories.'

The story depended on the photography. Schwartzmann wanted one picture and it was terribly simple: a portrait of three checky faces together around the boardroom table with Mr Fonzei. Rodney had said that, in view of the quality of writer, photographer and magazine, this coup could probably be arranged; they all simply had to watch and await their opportunity, and he would be strategic on their behalf.

So the journalist had waited. He came to the house now, he believed, like a trusted confederate, and was no longer challenged by Mr Fonzei's doorman (doormen were never part of having fun). From ten in the morning, when hope for the house seemed to renew in the smell of cleaning-wax, he remained until five, sharing the couch next to Rodney with angelic girls full of opium; with disc-jockeys who had shining fringes, withered eyes and an incapacity to sound the vowel 'ou'; with tramps and Buddhists (tramps in sheets) and dill-water youths who, though they came from Ilford, belonged to that incalculable mass of British dill-water Pop music that pretends to be American.

The journalist had witnessed the smoking of marijuana. Without difficulty he had mastered the lexicon of three or four phrases by which the ornaments of the office occasionally conversed. Their sentiments, he noticed, were invariably connected with a tremendous

131

concentration of power and great deeds to be achieved tomorrow. On several occasions, too, he had even believed himself to have an appointment, with the Bat or Mr Fonzei; but each time, the matter would be re-introduced by Rodney in the afternoon as one of hope and luck and sleight of hand.

At times he felt himself slipping, spinning into that deep coma which attends reliance upon the will of people who do not care either way, but now suddenly again it all looked hopeful. Schwartzmann the photographer arrived; a scraggy midget carrying, so as to be perfectly inconspicuous, a Strobe bulb and complaining of mouth ulcers. Schwartzmann was taken upstairs to catch Mr Fonzei outside the boardroom directly the meeting finished.

The journalist bucked up. 'Ugh,' he said, 'I'm never going to work with—that Schwartzmann's such a horrible bloody pessimist.'

Rodney sipped from one of the heavy-bottomed crystal glasses which, in twinkling rallies, still balanced half-empty on most of the sofa-backs. Fun must last as long as Coca Cola can be wasted; as long as cigarette ends float in whisky. 'I think Schwartzmann's an optimist,' Rodney said.

'You heard all that "I'm not this sort of photographer, I like spending six weeks with people" . . .'

'Schwartzmann's an optimist because he wants it all at once. You're the pessimist, Alan: you're grateful for every little thing.'

Like most parasites the journalist was flattered to be analysed. 'You're an optimist, Rodney.'

'Anybody scared for his job is an optimist.'

The journalist stared at him.

'At the moment,' Rodney said, 'you have to prove to Fonzei either that you're indispensable or harmless.

You're safe with Fonzei if he can say to you "You're shit, you know that, don't you: but this and this needs doing, get on with it."'

The journalist was genuinely shocked. As long as the legend had lived, hadn't Rodney always been there, answering the telephone humanely and wittily even in the great latter scandals, and the obsceneness of the writs? The house would probably fall tomorrow if not tonight. But surely that would just mean a change of office for Rodney. His peacock chair would be put somewhere else.

'You can fear and hate people,' Rodney said, 'and then they go and eat a peach and show you they're the same as you. They give you *some* kind of social behaviour. You say, "Got a cold then Mr so-and-so?" and he says, "Yes, shocking." But Fonzci just looks away. He won't admit he's got a cold.'

'—and yet,' Rodney added, 'I feel there must be a warm man there somewhere.' He said this on a curious lame note.

'Doesn't he have the saving grace—'

'The "saving grace"?'

'—of doing what he says he'll do?'

Rodney looked up at the ceiling.

'Oh, he'll screw EMI over the royalty-deal, yes.'

'But Rodney, for Christ's sake. You've all been getting screwed for years. You'll just get what you're entitled to in royalties. You'll trade profitably.'

Rodney murmured, 'But look at the friends it's cost us.' Suddenly the journalist saw that, on the contrary, he and Rodney had no *rapport*. Those dying pigeons, those timid plunderers around his chair or shaken out already into the street, Rodney thought of as *friends*.

The journalist, having arrived at this argumentative and slightly contemptuous point, was almost ready to withdraw. True, he had not managed to gain access to any figure of importance in the destiny of the house; that for an obituary might be so much the better. The phrases had began to clamour already in his mind. He needed no further dialogue, but only to know that Mr Fonzei had at last been photographed by Schwartzmann.

And one last formal question. 'Rodney, do you think Fonzei ever will get them to play together again?'

'Oh, think of it!' Rodney exclaimed.

'But I thought you said Fonzei was such a terrible liar.'

'I said he saw no difference between telling the truth and telling a lie. I said he never signs anything. But you know what his boast is: "I could make the deal that would settle Vietnam." You see, Alan, this is why Fonzei doesn't want The Bat to go to America. He couldn't have The Bat spoiling things—coming on by himself at some half-assed free concert, puffing away at a joint.'

'He couldn't stop The Bat going.'

'Not if The Bat had a visa, no.'

The desk intercom made the noise of a day-old chick. That, too, had once been fun. Rodney held the receiver off its stand.

'What the Americans say is that The Bat has been "guilty of a crime of moral turpitude". Alan—you actually get the man at Immigration saying, "You have been guilty of a crime of moral turpitude." The Bat just answers "turpentine"—wry Northern humour. What they *mean* is, they don't want him going over and giving film-shows of his bum again.

'Now they're at the stage of wanting to know *why* he wants to go. When you first came up here, Alan, you asked me what I did to justify my salary. I'll tell you. I fix it for The Bat to go to America because he wants to go to America; to see a few friends.'

At the intercom, on two notes, Rodney said, 'Hel-lo.'

He handed the journalist the receiver.

134

'It's Fonzei. For you.'

All of the Press Office telephones were now in use. The journalist still argued, kneeling up against the desk, and Rodney talked to Washington with his legs drawn up in his chair. Against the coloured walls, other figures stood at desks in the attitudes of intense listening that accompany the making of calls without offering to pay for them.

It was still raining; the girls, still waiting. It was five o'clock. At five, nothing—positively nothing is fun. Yesterday and tomorrow line up together at five, grinning hideously. At five, people are sacked. One may have an animal-skin coat—a face of wonderful alabaster—but at five o'clock, even youth ceases. One thing will get you by, however beautiful you are, and that is a cup of tea. Mr Fonzei had sacked the tea-lady.

Rodney was first to hang up. Much later the journalist put back the intercom receiver and, with a click of his knees, arose. The exertions of the conversation had soaked his jacket across the back.

'I love all trivia,' Rodney said. From close beside his desk, a monstrous airbrushed dervish head had appeared and was looking at the cigarette-case Rodney held out. 'See,' Rodney said, 'the inscription reads "From Irene to Alan, 1934".'

'Rodney do you *realize* how long that man's kept me on that—from the next *floor*! An hour?'

The door opened. Dolls recoiled in fear. It was Hazel. Rodney said, 'Fonzei has stopped The Bat from going to America.'

'Rodney: Delia's got in downstairs.'

'It looked so hopeful,' Rodney mused. 'The State Department said, all right they'd give him a visa *if* ... he stated the purpose of the visit was strictly business, but you see the application, in The Bat's case, also had

135

to be endorsed by the U.S. Department of Justice.'

'She's throwing wineglasses,' Hazel added.

'I was talking to our lawyer in Washington for an hour before I realized he wasn't our lawyer, he was Fonzei's lawyer. So Fonzei's lawyer has been negotiating on our behalf to have The Bat *refused* a visa, At least,' Rodney said, 'they'll only endorse his application if he's going over to make a speech at a mental-health conference.' Rodney sighed.

'Love—' the journalist entreated, 'has the meeting finished?'

'Oh yes,' Hazel remembered. 'Your friend. He's gone.'

'Gone!'

'The little one carrying the bulb, yeah.'

'*Gone!*'

'He said he wasn't going to hang about any more. He said to tell you he'd already waited an hour and fifty minutes while Mr Fonzei was on the phone; and he isn't that kind of photographer. He likes spending six weeks with people.'

The journalist said faintly, 'Oh, what a farce.'

And the marvel of it: who was responsible? Who had kept Mr Fonzei talking for an hour and fifty minutes?

Rodney put the cigarette case back in his drawer. 'A farce is what it used to be,' he said. 'In fact, it was very like a farce—remember you asked me to define this house, Alan? A farce with doors opening and shutting, people running about. But not an evil farce.'

All at once, with his soft, thick cuffs he lifted himself up on the arms of his chair, releasing to the view his shirt's full silk front and the breast of the embroidery, and the monogram. For the first time that the journalist could remember, Rodney raised his voice, which was scarcely raising it. 'Come on now, everybody, clear the room—clear the room please, I mean it.'

Rodney got up; the first time the journalist had seen

him out of his chair. A wild head lolled in surprise over the balcony of a couch nearby, but nobody moved, of the dead dolls in the room. On his stockinged feet Rodney walked through the beam of the projector, casting the shadow on the wall of a huge man pushing the hair from his eyes. He paused by the door, and stood and looked down at the ring of toy birds that still dipped their heads in a circle round the water-tray.

'Some of these birds' beaks are going mouldy,' he said. 'Nobody said they'd do that when we bought them. They cost us a pound each.'

The streets shone, all wet. The slewing taxis carried meters turned-down that glowed magically like lighted blackberries—taxis are still fun, money is still fun. On the third floor, above the line of windows with drawn blinds, all the lights were on; and from the doorstep the girls looked up and the lights reassured them.

Blues Next Door

Model A wore the gold; in his ear, his teeth, around his cigarette-holder and on the black rhino of one finger, his Creole ring. Asked why he chose to marry an English girl thirty-two years younger than himself, Model A replied, ''Cause in old-age I would prefer to smell perfume than liniment.' As for Sandra, her temper did not furnish reasons, she married him—so there! When Georgina was born, like perfect honey but slightly paralysed, it just seemed to make them hold hands tighter.

Sandra liked to say, 'He's part Cherokee as well, actually.' Further than that, no one dared to inquire: her hand, sudden-white on his, locked out all other difference. But she had been known to admit, 'Well, at first the language was—you know, a bit much. Because when all them Blues musicians get together, it's nothing but mother-this and mother-that—'

People had always called her sarcastic. Indeed, the more timid of her relatives could picture Sandra only in retort—hair backcombed from a somewhat angelic forehead, eyes drawn together, mouth puckered to a tart little trumpet. They could scarcely have imagined her as she was when she and Model A played about on the sofa, or when she nudged him and said, 'Tell us about New Orleans, Model.'

'I told you already a hundred times,' he teased, ''bout New Or-*leens*.'

'Tell us some more, go on.'

So he told her about the street gang he used to run in, who wore Indian feathers and lit bonfires in the street. He was named Model A for running faster than the police cars. And when the Chief passed by, he told her with his eyes wide, all of them used to sit down in the road and stop the traffic. There was a white boy from Georgia—this phrase awakening enemy bells forty years later in the white girl from Matlock, Derbyshire— who tried to drive through and was whipped by the gang with axes.

Ooh, but he had his moods. Anything might set him off, Sandra noticed; the most commonplace home sound, like a clack of the wooden dog-gate or Georgina's footsteps pummelling across the room above. His moustache went lumpy as if he had a mouthful of boiled sweets; she was even a little frightened of the cuts that appeared all over his face.

'Forget about all that,' she urged him, 'come on, duck.'

'I cain't forget 'bout it. All my life from six years old, all I ever wanted,' he mumbled, 'was to work and save enough money and git enough ammunition and catch them Kluxers in a meetin' and spray 'em and let 'em spray me, 'long as I could lie down in the field with a few of 'em, I'd be happy.'

Sandra tried to be patient. But she found it hard to picture Model A smaller than he now was, let alone watching his mother and father burn to death. How could it still haunt him, on a Council estate? And Georgina climbed on his knees to swing the boxing-gloves from another part of his past that hung on the wall. 'She wants to play the piano like Dadda, don't you? Oh, go on Model, show her.'

'—all o' that was buildin' up in me ever' day from

eight years old. Them Kluxers burn the church too.
Jesus—he came from the arabs' country, *he* wasn't no
white man.

'Christmas, nobody give you nothin'. I used to go to
a show on Christmas. Sit up in that show till ever' thing
finish. Christmas for me 'jus' like any other of the
days...'

'*Get* on!' Sandra chided. She'd heard this one so many
times.

'I mean it. Jus' like any other of the days.'

'Oooh!' she exclaimed. 'You lousy cow! You *know*
you enjoy shopping for Georgy at Christmas as much as
I do. Every year it's the rotten same. "Oh, we're not
going to spend so much this year" and we always finish
up spending forty pound.'

They lived on his savings. Though the house was
small for four—Sandra's Dad as well—Model A had
bought it from the Council. That, and his van lettered
'Model A Statesborough, Blues Singer of New Orleans'
gave them a prestige on the Estate, because the van was
brand-new. They lived surrounded by all that was normal at home to Sandra: bits of dropped food, nail-
varnish bottles, Georgina's socks drying like tiddlers on
the cage of the gas-fire. Model A liked system, however,
and finally prevailed with it. On the kitchen-wall an
envelope hung below the notice 'All the paying-off books
is *here*'. He never kept her short. Money was no part
of this present exasperation.

The North of England's deepest dislike is of any kind
of waste. Sandra's uncertainty as to the precise commodity
being wasted made it all the more tantalizing to her:
the entreaties by succeeding posts that Model A should
go back to singing and playing. The BBC in Leeds even
sent telegrams—a telegram signified most vital urgency
to her—but all he said was, 'No, I ain't gonna hire
myself to nobody no more.'

143

'Then,' Sandra yelled, 'you're barmy, aren't you!'

And there were the people who turned up on the doorstep to see him, looking as if they'd walked across the world, which in some cases they had; Sandra hauled them inside quickly before the neighbours saw.

For these, however peculiar they were, Model A always gave in and played the old piano upstairs wedged against the bars of Georgina's cot. They sat in a row in the cot with their mouths open like baby birds. Since they always looked half-starved, he'd cook a meal for them too; he was a good cook. Eating ham-hocks and string beans and rice with a view across the recreation ground to the power-station, their faces changed, as Sandra put it, 'from dreamy to plain daft'.

But what nettled her most of all was the man who claimed to have every record Model A had ever made; over two hundred of them. The huge old breakable ones—like those Sandra had thrown out when Elvis Presley started—no one but the collector himself was allowed to touch. She asked how much they were worth and he said, eighty or ninety pounds each. Her campaign was renewed that night.

'—no, I ain't gonna hire myself no more.'

'Oooh!' She could shake him. He was little enough.

'It's not of interes' to *no*body,' he said.

'They're all begging for you, you great lump!'

Model A showed the gold in his teeth.

'"They",' he repeated, 'who "they"? Huh? "They" just the jivers and cheaters. All "they" want to do is jive you after they use you. "They" 'llowed Blind Lemon Jefferson to die at the streetcar stop.'

'Now don't start mithering on about Blind Lemon Jefferson again.'

'—he lie next to Classie in a unmarked grave. You know who done put him in there? "They."'

'It's different,' she urged, 'it's England.'

Then he said something that really made her wild.

'Aah, you white folks is all the same—'

'You'll pay for it, you know that, don't you?' Sandra shouted after him, up stairs that were hung with photographs of him at the microphone on tropic nights before she was born.

She turned to Mrs Trolley their neighbour who, by an infallible radar for violence or celebration, had appeared at the side-door in a turban.

'He'll pay for it, he will,' Sandra told her. 'He always does when he's sorry. I got a new pair shoes out of him last time.'

Both their stomachs were upset, the day Big Sister Oak came. Model A's cure for any illness, taught to him by the Italian Orphanage in New Orleans fifty years ago, was a hot potion of rum and garden-mint; and Sandra had spent an unhappy morning on the couch in little grimacing curses, trying to bring it up again as wind. Dad was there too, watching the Persian lessons on television.

Model A started to mend her electric hair-rollers. He was, in every direction, clever round the house; he did the ironing and fed Georgina on Sandra's two mornings at work. Only in some ordinary thing like this did Sandra ever feel the twitch of something uncommon in her life; or when he looked over the day's runners at York with his cigarette-holder in his mouth, or took his shirt off to wash, and she saw the brown glisten of his prize-fighting scars.

Like all houses in those parts, their side-door remained open, to admit neighbours, neighbours' children, the large-tail dogs peculiar to small dwellings. But as a rule any visitor was signalled by Mrs Trolley—Radio Ambury, Model A called her as this was Ambury Park Estate. Sandra's eyes were closed with a spasm and at first she didn't realize someone had come in. She merely thought the sun had clouded over.

Rex the Alsatian jumped from under the table. Model A looked up from the point of his screwdriver. Normally, reading-glasses gave his face an old man's scowl but Sandra now saw it change—as it sometimes did if he sang his rude song to Georgina in the bath—to a little boy's, with dimples tightened by invisible lemons.

'Hey—'

Rex alerted his ears, but decided not to bark.

'Hey,' said a voice, 'there's a dog outside! Go see thuh dog!'

Sandra turned round.

'Oh hel-*lo*, Big Sister Oak. Come in, my duck.'

Big Sister Oak chuckled at Rex, who was cowering under the table, 'Hey, that guy don' know he's a dog. Go on brother, go see thuh dog outside.'

She doffed her Army tunic and changed from men's work shoes to flat-heel slippers. Above the incalculable mass of her flowered pinafore, a tiny face glowed as if it cooked in plums.

'I'm sweatin' already,' said Big Sister Oak, ' 'scuse me, gen'lemen.'

'One egg or two, Big Sister Oak?'

'Model A,' she replied jovially, ' 'splain to this young bitch, I got to have *six* eggs fo' breakfast.'

Georgina knelt on the little stool and watched. The Cherokee ancestors had left such graceful bones in her, there seemed no more to the disability than a pretty obliqueness, until her mother ordered, 'Use your other hand, Georgy.'

She never left Big Sister Oak all that day—riding on the hip of the pinafore mountain, climbing the broad elastic leg to tumble flop! like a trampoline into Big Sister's Oak's lap. They walked together over the Rec-

146

reation Ground, the honey child and a monument in carpet-slippers. Sandra looked out of the window. They were still together in the sand-pit.

Later she asked Big Sister Oak, 'Is Shut Eye down in London with you?'

'No he ain't. You know, Model A—las' thing, they done stole Shut Eye's gitar.'

'They *stole* his *gitar*!'

'Sho' nuff. While he's sleepin' on the subway train.'

'Hell.'

'He's funny, he is,' Sandra said fondly. 'Just goes off for forty winks when he feels like it.'

'—when he wake up—*my*! The subway train in the yard and the gitar gone!' Big Sister Oak's eyes widened at Georgina. 'But Shut Eye still leanin' on it!'

'Oooh, Big Sister Oak, you ought to have seen the pair of them when Shut Eye came up here. He gave Georgina twenty dollars when he went. No, it was forty, wasn't it, Model? Forty dollars he gave her.'

'You never drank no liquor, did you?' Big Sister Oak inquired.

Model A innocently shook his head. On the sofa next to her, with his little boy's face he sat up all straight and dimpled. Big Sister Oak belonged to the second generation of Blues singers who could only think of him as a little waif from the Italian Orphanage, and who disapproved of his drinking spirits. The last time Sandra had seen her—in Copenhagen just before Model A stopped playing the Continental clubs—Big Sister Oak sternly declined a glass of gin on his behalf.

Later in the evening, a rash Dane had hit her with a chair. Big Sister Oak was unmoved. She then threw the Dane through a closed double set of folding-doors.

'—but I was plenty gone that night on Long Life beer,' Model A said mischievously. Dad's ears went back like a gundog's at the word 'beer'.

'Oooh, he's not kidding an' all. Him and Shut Eye was paralytic-drunk together that night—lousy cow!'

'I enjoy a drink,' Dad remarked.

Sandra narrowed her eyes at Model A.

'Don't you sit there pulling that innocent face. Oooh! —he comes upstairs, and I'm chasing him all round the room trying to rotten-well undress him and all the time he's on the move. He wouldn't stop still. Shall I tell you what happened then?'

'Yeah, hit it, Little Mama,' Big Sister Oak said genially.

'—well, here's me wakin' up at five o'clock in the morning and he's hanging on to me—weren't you?— yelling "Don't let him get me, don't let him get me!" Know what it was? He'd been reading the book *Dracula*, and thought Dracula was coming to get him.'

In the afternoon, Sandra took Big Sister Oak into town to try to find her a dress at Pack's. No dress would fit her, of course, nor confederacy of dresses; but behind the full laundry-bags of her breast there beat a schoolgirl's heart. She loved to bring her dainty flat nose all the way down to smell different perfumes dabbed on the forearm of a salesgirl whose face, while this was happening, remained immobile as a trapped hare's.

'What's the name o' that one, honey?'

'*Rose of Autumn*,' the girl managed to say.

'Back home, we had a rose,' Big Sister Oak remarked. ' 'Reckon why that smelt so good was we pee on it ever' day.'

Several times during her visit, she intimated that she wanted Model A to join her Blues show in London. 'I got to get me a good Blues *man*—I don't want no chile.' But he turned it aside or said no one was interested in him.

'Nobody *interested*?' Big Sister Oak repeated.

Sandra burst out, 'And how many rotten telegrams

have you had from the BBC, eh, you great lump?'

'That mean, nobody *interested* in T Bone,' Big Sister Oak said, 'or Muddy Waters or The Spoon—'

'—chap down in London spends a fortune ringing up saying "When's he going to appear, when's he going to appear?"'

'Nobody *interested*?' Big Sister Oak said incredulously. 'You know—one time he playin' in a joint with *bad* cats there. While he playin', a guy gits five shells in the kisser from a forty-five—ring, ring, rap against the bar-rail—'

'Oh, leave him,' Sandra said in exasperation. 'He's got it into his thick head people are going to try and cheat him.'

'Five shots,' Big Sister Oak said. 'The shooter runs out, the po lice runs in. "Hey, who was that shooter—what was that shooter like?" All the people in the bar say "Hell, he was just a man, had a gun, he was just a killer, c'mon Model A and play. Whup that piano, Mr Piano-Whupper!"'

When Big Sister Oak's taxi came, the sun was ripe on the pavement: so were Mrs Trolley, her friend Mrs Tattman, Mrs Tattman's daughter-in-law's baby Tania, and across the road, all down the hill, all sorts of people suddenly found it necessary to open their front-bedroom windows.

Georgina brought flowers from the garden for her—buttercups, pansies and Michaelmas daisies, their stems all hot with the clutch of love. Big Sister Oak lowered the dress-circle of her chin; Georgina reflected buttercups in it. Then, in front of all the neighbours she lifted Georgina up, and up further with the buttercups too, and kissed her all over, in every place where she was not quite perfect.

Just before she drove off she said, 'Model A—I been

keepin' it from you—' but what it was, Sandra couldn't hear, because Georgina suddenly burst into tears. Only when they were back in the house—how dull it seemed and how spacious—did he tell her:

'Shut Eye dead.'

'You *what*!'

He'd died of pneumonia. That, to Sandra, was the curious part; she always imagined it boiling-hot in America. And he'd been sweet, too: bringing home half the butcher's for them every day, giving Georgina forty dollars, going happily off to sleep on the rug.

Model A said nothing more. He put his spectacles back on: the cheeky face vanished. He finished mending her hair-rollers, then he went upstairs. In Georgina's room, the piano started chopping.

Dad, meanwhile, had risen from a television-programme concerning potters' wheels, and was pulling on his cardigan. All day, to the overflowing of Big Sister Oak he had awarded no more attention than to anyone who dropped in—Dad sat immovably beside the television, peering round at it as if viewing for a moment under sufferance. By night, however, he conducted one of the authentically beautiful relationships a man can have with the highlights in a glass of bitter.

Sandra was brisk. She got Mrs Trolley to come in and sit with Georgina: she made Model A go with Dad for a drink and take her along as well. She did her best to be cheerful, but he looked really old this evening; his eyes were speckled like bird's eggs with pink, his voice thickened almost too much even for her to understand. What he drank was a bad sign, too—beer and white wine together, like the stevedores of New Orleans.

'Real character, isn't she, though?' Sandra said. 'Remember when she threw that Danish chap through the folding-doors?'

'He lucky she never slit his gizzard.'

Then Model A relapsed into what he had been mumbling earlier, '—through Hell for me, that cat went. Through Hell—'

'Who did, love? Shut Eye?'

'He coulda cried himself, at what the Kluxers done.'

'Well, come on then,' she said with energy. 'Talk about it. Trouble shared is trouble halved. Tell Dad about when you was on the boxcars.'

'—and Otis Spann, he came over, went back and died —Sonny Boy Williamson came over, went back and died —Bukka White—'

'Oh Model, don't be morbid, love.'

'I mean it,' he said. ' 'Scare me to death, these cats with all o' their dyin'.'

Dad winked at the healing golds in his glass.

'Y'only die once,' he remarked.

They were at a new pub called The Crazy Horse— a smoky lake of beer with tables like damp, red lily-pads and columns round the edge where the local yobs leaned with an assumed air of expectancy. Full— thundery in the chip of bottles, it was still no place for trouble. Wrestlers were employed, clearing pint-glasses like rings on their fingers, there was usually a cabaret and the police had proved they could, only seconds after an alarm, effect a grand trampling entrance with Alsatians.

Trouble in bars was of the distant past anyway, to Sandra: four years ago when she met him. He had mellowed since, thanks to home and little Georgina and the local ale; and put his knife away in a pocket of his best suit. It was Sandra who dealt with any bother when they were out—not much of it round here. Should a philosopher accuse Model A of coming and taking white people's jobs, she, with mouth-fatiguing scorn, would reply, 'Yes, and he's stole one of your women, too, and what you going to do about it?'

Sandra caught the laugh—a scrap of beery filth from that clout of yobs round the pillar—but not the remark which provoked it. She never did discover what accidental hooks caught and bore it over the ale smoke to Model A, right into the part of his brain where violence endured despite four years of taking the dog out.

The first she knew was his chair falling.

Through the tables and legs and rallied glasses to the side of the room, a broad aisle had opened. At the altar of it, the yobs stood back impressed at the one of their number who was crucified cosily a short way up the pillar by Model A's knee, and all eyes pooled in the adoration of fear at the blade of Model A's knife: for he happened to be wearing his best suit tonight.

'Breathe loud,' he said, 'and I'll pull y'dam head off.'

So she won. He had to play once more in case he unexpectedly died; he kept to this theme with big eyes, despite Sandra's hilarity.

But on the night itself she was the one to be tense. There was the smell of nerves in the pear-drops of her nail-polish. And Georgina was grizzly, and Mrs Trolley took a misguidedly humorous viewpoint and kept getting in the way on the stairs and curtseying. Round the van outside, a small crowd waited.

'Model! Where'd you get that shirt from?'

'Just under th'other shirts,' he said calmly.

'It's a mass of wrinkles!'

'Well, what kinda' place is this we goin'?'

'How should I know?' she blazed.

'You wanted it.'

'*I* wanted it. I like that! Who thinks he's going to drop down dead on the doormat!'

'How much they fixin' to pay us?'

'Twelve,' she said, 'and a percentage of the takings over and above so much, I made sure of that with the feller, he sounded ever so nice, so don't you start wittering about "they're trying to cheat me", all right, my lad?'

Then her father came downstairs. His best sports-jacket was mantled by a shirt of horrendous vermilion.

'Just the job to knock around in,' he remarked with satisfaction.

'But you're not *going* to knock around—oh Dad, honestly!' Like most women of thirty, Sandra was deeply formal in her habits.

Calmer in her trouser-suit, she said, 'Come on then, let's put your earring in.'

But it kept falling out. Model A's lobe had slackened so far in all the years since it was pierced, when the practice survived from tabulation of cotton slaves.

'Keep it in your pocket-book 'till I begin playin',' he suggested.

Outside the club his name appeared, incorrectly spelled, between two Yorkshire rock groups of no consequence with romantic North American sobriquets.

It was as dark as a cinema inside. All that showed was the white figure of a disc-jockey who danced above their heads while an earthquake acclaimed him—whistles—cries that he should never, ever stop—and he, for his part, embraced the blackness that adored him, he stretched, he writhed, he ground his tightened buttocks one upon another.

When Sandra's eyes had absorbed the first walls of night, she saw that in fact nobody in the club was applauding—the customers stood around with arms dismally folded since, with the ovation, it was impossible to dance. The ovation was played on a record. The triumph of fame in which the disc-jockey whirled had no source but his own opinion of himself.

They were taken to a banquette beside a harsh break in the darkness lettered 'Service Door'. A moment later the owner of the club passed; or Sandra concluded that it was. He wore a business suit and stiff collar upon which the bluey bar-twilight luminously played. He did not acknowledge their presence.

She put her irritation aside, however, in sizing up the complete strangers who had surrounded them and begun to talk to Model A. Two boys, dressed in what looked to her like school paint-rags, sat on either side of him, tossing their heads, staring at his mouth when he spoke. Since Dad had assumed on the promontory of the banquette, the attitude of reclining Nero, the other fellow had to kneel down—a kneeling face since he wore all black. He was the Londoner; the photographer who had been ringing them up for months.

'All right, I don't mind having a half,' Dad said graciously, but otherwise, the conversation was not easy.

'I didn't get you,' Model A said brusquely.

'Socks taught you the Blues, isn't that right?'

'Are those cowboy boots you're wearing?' Sandra asked the photographer.

'But what was he like? Socks?'

'Alcoholic,' said Model A.

'I tell you,' Model A said to her—and the rest of them strained forward to hear, 'I ain't so appointed of Georgina stoppin' the whole night with Radio Ambury.'

'All right then—clever! How do we get out for the evening, if Mrs Trolley doesn't look after her?'

'I jus' don't want for her to get too enthused so she forgets where her real home is.'

'Model A—' pleaded the face.

'Yeah,' he said ironically.

'Your grandfather did play on the riverboats with King Oliver, didn't he—?'

Presently the disc-jockey became temporarily sated

with adoration. Across the dance-floor, he now appeared to be playing at shops behind an area of glass. A confused announcement bearing upon 'The Living Legend,' began. Model A stood up. There were people on their knees all round him.

'My earring!' he exclaimed.

'All right, hold still, I ain't got rubber-arms—'

Sandra kept their places while he played. She'd heard it all for years—that chopping piano up in Georgina's room. She ate a basket of chips, which, despite the eccentricities of the place, were not at all bad. She looked at the time or tested a loose rosette on her shoe. Beside her, motionless and ale-pink, Dad reclined, beatific as a moored balloon.

'How'd it go, duck?' she said when Model A came back.

'All right.'

The club had changed. The darkness had been intensified before by apathy. Now that it was packed to the archways, all the lights glimmered half-on and awash somehow, like the aftermath of tears or a pub at chucking-out time.

There was applause, but this time the disc-jockey couldn't turn it down. The disc jockey's voice, indeed, drowned somewhere behind the scenes.

'—will you all carry on dancing now, *please*—'

Model A sat down. Every crease in his shirt had vanished.

'All right, Dad?' He gave a sudden, huge smile, then he laughed. 'Dad only here for de beer.'

'Bloody Hell!' stammered a voice. 'I've never heard anything remotely like it!'

'Did you see the way he handled that trio?'

'Lovely—pecking—light—not a note too many. Stone me!'

'I know what long hair's for; I've suddenly realized.

It's to shake and shake across your face when you hear a thing like that—'

'He played the guitar as well—'

The guitarist knelt among the others. He held up the red electric biscuit as if he disbelieved what sounds had been won from it.

One of the boys in paint-rags, the leader of the local trio who had accompanied Model A, pleaded, 'Were we really all right, do you think?'

'Now I know how you tell great music—'

'How about that *Wine Wine Wine?*'

'—And *The Sheikh of Araby.*'

'—it's when an audience sings along *in tune!*'

'Model!' Sandra exclaimed. 'You showed me up!'

The Sheikh of Araby was the rude song he sometimes sang to Georgina in the bath.

Model A leaned forward as Sandra wiped his forehead glowing like a mahogany bedknob. She could tell he was in a lovely mood: when all the lines in his face, under the grey peak of curls, looked so kind that he became the father she needed as well as the husband.

'Look,' he said, 'you got a i-dea. I gotta say this for the ben'fit of the local musicians that was with me there. 'Long as you have an i-dea, ain't no-*body* play any better'n you all.'

'Eh, do you really mean it?'

The sigh the paint-rag heaved was broader than his body.

It was the disc-jockey, in fact, who came across to speak to them about payment; the twelve pounds and the percentage. That percentage must be due: the club was packed, even though its customers all now no longer knew what to do with themselves. Nobody moved, nobody danced to the faint strivings of tin that came through the loud-speakers but somewhere they were still singing *The Sheikh of Araby* with Model A's descant:

—at night when you're asleep
           with no pants on
—in-to your tent I'll creep
           with no pants on

The emissary was shorter than might have been sup-
posed from below his pedestal, and his romper suit of
white was not absolutely spotless.

With a radiant smile he said, 'Can you just come back
into the, er, office Model A, my love?'

'I told you,' Sandra said, 'I'm dealing with that part
of it, all right?'

'—Model A, how many versions of *Frankie and Johnny*
are there?'

'I been told, ten thousand.'

'I don't mind a half,' Dad's voice answered.

'I'm not your love either,' Sandra crisply informed
the disc-jockey.

When she returned from the office, she had to fight
to get through to Model A.

'It really stood in a graveyard!'

Around him the faces rocked in an ecstasy of New
Orleans and the agonies of kneeling.

'Sho's Hell in a graveyard,' Model A agreed. 'Back
o'Chantilly we know it as.'

'Fantastic!'

'Ever' day we see 'em tippin' the dead people in
to the—'

'*Right*, that's the finish! Excuse me, please. Come on,
Dad, we're going home now.

'You know how much they reckon they took at the
door,' she stormed, 'eighty-one pound! We get a percentage after a hundred, he's charging fifty pence each to
get in and the place is rotten-well packed. I'm going to
look at his book.

'Do you know what I said to him? I said "You're the

lowest of the low, and you know what that is, don't you! It's the snake that crawls in the grass." '

'I don' want it,' Model A said.

'Doesn't matter what *you* rotten-well want, I'm going to see his book. Eighty-one pound I don't think! '

'Drop this now, Sandy, you hear?'

He only called her that in dead earnest.

'—talk about low, tight-fisted, mean, grasping—'

'Honey,' he said pacifically, 'that's the Jive.'

He took his cigarette-holder up to his mouth with his gold ring, and suddenly she thought: it's beneath him.

'Here—no diff'ent,' Model A said. 'Same jive. You freezin' like Blind Lemon Jefferson at the streetcar-stop and they—they sorry—they only took eighty-one pound. We don't got to play for 'em.'

In the heart of the young crowd, he shrugged.

'Only thing is, we got to.'

Out in the cold air, Dad yawned so vastly that Sandra had to warn him the wind might change. He altered it to musical yawns in ascending and descending scales. The trio of paint-rags who had accompanied Model A were loading their equipment into an old ambulance—he walked over and pulled a door back and grinned up at them and they grinned down at him and it was safe and secret between them, the cleverness implied in the use of an old ambulance. Sometimes, she thought, she'd never understand him.

Half-way home Model A said, 'Nex' time I play that club I gonna go there *without* my wife.'

Sandra replied, 'What they want there, my lad, is a young cock not an old rooster.' But under boats of the city-light, they touched hands a moment.

The Finish of the Stars

✳

Certain apartments faced out of the ghetto by fissures in it: these saw the sun set, downtown. From others there might be no prospect but a wall the colour of dried blood, yet still, between the fire-ladders, every window had opened. Cushions drooped on the sills, elbows knelt on the cushions as people took the imprisoned air sweetly on their eyes.

And they brought out kitchen chairs to the stoops or settled down on the plump stone ruin of a balustrade. Freedom was in abatement of the wind which all day had flapped garbage up like buzzards from the corner. Life went free in a broom, a boy's shoes, the pile of steam from a vent as the drains, too, sighed.

Release and happiness were the nights that Pearl Aiken played her Africa records, loud. A bass bumping opened electric lilies of a guitar. They looked upward, they leaned farther out; and through Pearl's open window, the voice of Timmie Royale filled the street with a sigh of luxury, a giggle of worship for someone handsome.

When Timmie sleepily snarled, they could see her face with a bunch of wet liquorice curls beside it. But as the voice lifted, they saw her arms. Her mink arms stretched above them, beyond clay and iron and skylights and even the weight of the sky itself, with her rose-coloured palms held flat as if to feel the finish of the stars.

It was a song Timmie said she never wanted to stop singing. It belonged to all of them: to Pearl Aiken, to the boy dancing on a broom, to the old man with cigars in his shirt, who danced. It celebrated the city Negro, out and strolling proud in his greatest shark skin clothes. He had never been seen in this city; they could only picture him in Africa music. But the spring of the dream, they knew, was themselves. Africa Records was theirs, no white man could steal it, fourteen blocks across town.

Like many cities without hope, this one was popular as a convention-centre. At the moment it belonged to the Grailers, a freemasonry whose purpose is to wear little blue embroidered skullcaps. Their official jubilations had ended with the parade this afternoon—there were still skullcaps all over Rovira Circle, however, standing round the pink civic fountains, in rollicksome groups under a marquee or shouting at the piano-player in cocktail-lounges. All the store-windows still said 'Welcome Grailers' behind their steel cages.

Not a grand parade, a big, grand, white parade, a parade, it was of wonderful, prodigal, pointless toys thickly-hung with middle-aged men; for the secondary purpose of the Grailers is to horse around like nobody's business. Down Estrella Avenue came the first waves, past the Church of the Annunciation and the Africa Records building—midget racing-cars with the drivers' stomachs resting outside, weaving and shrieking patterns across the boulevard; midget jalopies and motor-cycles all but o'ertoppled by the sportive bulk of their riders; and next, the decorated paddy-wagons flaming with escutcheons of the Cincinnati, Toledo or Sepulpa Grailers and crowned with the high officials of these chapters and their wives, bowing vinously at black faces that watched; then—oh!

Mounted Arabs and drills of Zouaves, files of white and blue and middle-aged West Point cadets; flocks of plains Indians carrying the Stars and Stripes with no trace of irony, formations of high-step drum majors switching the blades of their wands; Turks in curly slippers from Barstow, Texas; men-at-arms in chain mail from Albuquerque; and crazy and military and Dixieland bands; swollen-headed clowns who fired balloons from mortars, who lifted and set down feet as long as skis; clowns from the most patriotic Grailer chapters of the Midwest; Mickey Mouse, Pluto, Donald Duck, with vast chortling cheeks and eyes; and Donald Duck again.

Another Donald Duck. Another scream of miniature cars, beaming presidents, horses and rustled flags—everything in fact, endlessly repeated from the spiritless sun towards the hags of old skyscrapers, so that presently all of it seemed to originate, not in the play-park on South Estrella, but in some lower region of the earth, some Hell of trick-cycling. And, behind the Police barriers, the black faces, continuous and immobile, watched the green faces, the whisky-bruised or silver star-dust faces and the Dixieland bands. Grailers are, as stated, a white fraternity. Now there passed by a fourth Donald Duck. Stopping beside a black child seated on an angle of the barricades, riotously he bowed. The child burst into tears.

But a holy peace had descended at last, cocktail-hour. The painted parade stood in Rovira Circle around the pink fountains, unattended. Estrella was deserted—dead signs and shuttered luncheonettes passing away to twilight. The sun disappeared behind the Sheraton Pontiac Hotel. In its last moments it woke every facing window with light.

At the top of the Africa Records building on Estrella Avenue, one short domino of light remained. Pearl Aiken and some friends, pausing outside for as long as was wise at night on South Estrella, looked up and imagined all of them—Timmie, Little Alphonse, the Ultimates gesturing as if with lighted almonds at the finger-ends—but none of the stars were there any more. Pearl Aiken's dreams fluttered against what in effect was a warehouse. All the recording side had been moved out to the West Coast a year ago.

The light shone in the office of Mrs Ramona Trickett, executive-vice-president of Africa Records, who was signing cheques for building-maintenance. After a moment, Mrs Trickett rose, changed from her slippers into her shoes and put on her coat and hat. She wished good-night to her brother, the founder and president of the corporation, whose bearded face watched from a sentimental frame on her desk. Mrs Trickett kept all his school report-cards, too, in a drawer.

It was by the presence of a guard that mystery still dwelt in the Africa Records building—a guard wearing the livery of the small army which guarded Mrs Trickett's brother from all eyes in Beverly Hills. But at six-thirty the guard went home. The security of the thousands of stored album-sleeves passed to George, a most correct and quiet old switchboard-man. As Mrs Trickett let herself out of the ancient elevator-cage, he half-rose from his desk.

'Did you see the parade, George?' she said.

'Yes, 'night Mis' Trickett.' George nodded hugely. 'Oh *yes*, Mis' Trickett, I surely did see that.'

He held the slug of the phone-headset to his ear in puzzlement, as if being hailed from far off.

'I got a *call*, Mis' Trickett . . .'

If people still attempted to ring up their dreams at Africa Records, it was to George that they talked.

'It's a child, Mis' Trickett. Sayin' she want to speak with Little Alphonse, and I says, "You wastin' your time 'cause he's in *Lost* Angeles. They *all* in Lost Angeles 'cept Mis' Trickett and me." And she says, "Well, mister, just you give me Alphonse's number at home in Lost Angeles." I said, "Why I cain't do that, by the rules." '

He looked so cute there at his desk. He had a bright, soft, moon-lipped face like Bo Jangles, she thought, in the old photographs.

'The child said to me,' continued George, ' "Why that'll be all right 'cause I was just speakin' with Alphonse a minute ago" and I says to her, "Why, if you was speakin' with Little Alphonse, then how come you don't got his number to phone?" And you know what *she* said, Mis' Trickett?'

'Uh-uh.' She smiled, for she was a kind woman, at this pert child's airy command of the top-selling Africa artist around the world.

'She says to me, "That's okay 'cause when I was just speakin' with Little Alphonse," ' George repeated, wide-eyed, ' "he was in the bath-tub." She said his Mamma had caught him usin' the phone in the bath-tub and had made him hang up!'

At last he touched the kick-lock under his desk. The double-doors slid apart: it was not Timmie Royale who came out of the building this time, but a lady in a hat and coat. George settled back again with his paper, the telephone mouth-piece waving slightly in front of him as he turned a page. The building was silent, but for the hum of the soft-drinks dispenser.

Above George's peaceful head the corporation emblem, a big, succulent letter A, filled the wall. Around it, in a photo-montage, crowded all the Africa artists—Timmie, The Ultimates, Alphonse with his blind boy, sunglass grin, soloists smiling and laughing, groups like the Princes of Africa in laughing antics: all were there.

All wore the collars and wigs of a year ago. High on show-billboards now, above the white Californian freeways, each of them looked quite different.

His day's activity had coated the boy, his peanut head, his clothes and their holes, in a thick dusting of chalk. Mesmerized by the Grailer wagon on its trailer, he nevertheless couldn't stand still. He circled round and completed one very swift passage over the tarpaulin covering it. He marched, elbows flying, beside it, jiving in exultation of the pink fountains reflected in its brilliant yellow sides. He danced away on his stringy shoes, he came back to peer at his own eyes whitening to left and right in the shining brass headlamp. Then he grabbed the lamp.

They were on him in a moment. A large group had been standing only yards away under the Sheraton Pontiac marquee, cutting up old scores; for good times are so hard to bring to an end. Two Grailers in fatherly-looking plaid shirts and skullcaps caught hold of the boy; a third wearing the emblem of the Walla Walla (Washington) chapter began punching and slapping him: in the lip, the kidneys, at the weakness of his thin, black arms and on the forehead. As they worked, to their great amusement, a cloud of chalk arose.

This was not, however, the origin of the riots. Nor was it the policeman shot at June Street and Estrella, nor the policeman shot in a suburb while attending a false alarm, nor the two black queens who fell from a window on St Botolph, through a rotting balcony, fighting to the death. That the affair should come to be known as the Grailer riots was not quite appropriate since those jolly men, at the first hush of paint-flame among their vehicles, left the city at once. But it helps to give a disaster a nickname. It is the simplest way of putting officialdom in the right.

166

To locate the actual glow-worm would never have been possible. The riot had already been scheduled for some weeks; its participants recruited and reimbursed by a limited company of men who bore a striking resemblance to artists' impressions of them in the police manuals. They, too, quickly left the city, quickly but with the warm confidence of skilled craftsmen.

So it was that Colonel Howard 'Gus' Burlingame, driving home from the National Guard Armoury after the weekend's exercises, answered his police radio just as he was approaching his exit for the suburbs. Another moment and it would have been too late.

When he heard it, he exclaimed, 'Good gosh, I'm all excited!'

'Uh-uh, not me!' Laverne shook her head. Black curls puffed on all sides of it, so violently that her face appeared to rest between the paws of a very large bear. 'Uh-uh—I ain't fixing to make a million. To make a million with Africa—boy you gotta write a million.'

'Don't you aim to write a million?' the Prince inquired gravely.

'Aw but look!' Dot Sambrook resumed her complaint. She was English; blonde and more conspicuously white in the club for also dressing dingily in white. To the colony of Africa songwriters at the West Coast, she brought some of the anaemia of a Home Counties insurance clerk but, in collaboration with Laverne, had produced her share of song-hits.

'Look,' she said wearily, 'we wrote the thing for Little Alphonse!'

'It's not so serious,' Laverne said.

'But we wrote it for Alphonse, right?'

She turned to the Prince, who solemnly inclined towards her his ebony bullfrog head. He was seven feet tall and sang falsetto with The Princes of Africa; for

167

many years, poor relatives in the catalogue of Africa Records.

'We wrote a thing for Alphonse, see, to follow *Love Poem* and when he heard the tape he went out of his tree, right? Thought it was the greatest thing we'd ever done. Then Galahad tells us it's not Alphonse's kind of thing, right? And he'll go and stick it on some shit-heap—'

'Rel-ax,' Laverne said, 'grab some air.' It was more important to their partnership to woo the Prince. 'Hey, Otis—how long you all been with Africa Records for?'

'Seven years and a half,' replied the Prince. He looked modestly down at his grey top hat trimmed with ribbons of a Catholic purple.

'All on tour, huh?'

'Yes, on tour. We toured with Miss Royale and the Ultimates when they was one group. In the early days.'

'And Spody O'Dee?'

'*Right*,' the Prince said, grinning like a clean plate.

'Hey, you know!' Laverne said, wriggling. 'One time these guys was playin' a club like this—hey, where was it the guy starts in shootin' at you all, Otis?'

'In Corpus Christi, Texas,' the Prince replied.

'But ain't nobody gonna shoot you all now, huh?'

'I hope not,' said the Prince.

'—'cause you fin'lly got a hit record.'

'We fin'lly got a hit record.'

It was in celebration of this long-awaited event that the club was crushed full to see The Princes of Africa. The club associated itself, correctly, with the break-through; not realizing this would now free the Princes from the necessity of ever coming back.

Possibly the Princes themselves did not yet realize it yet—therefore Laverne and Dot Sambrook had swiftly flown in from Africa Records' new offices at the West Coast. They would beguile the Princes with new song-material and, if necessary, themselves. In the thrifty rule of their president, Mrs Trickett's brother, better than writing a group's next hit record was writing its next three or four.

'Where you all stayin' at?' inquired the Prince.

'The Marrakesh. And you know!' Laverne exclaimed. 'That's right up close to that little old tin shack!'

'On St Botolph, sure. That's where Africa Records got started.'

'You all came from round here, did you?' Dot Sambrook said listlessly.

'Hey, the Ultimates was just High School kids, right?'

The Prince nodded. 'From the Subotsky Housing Project right here in the north-west section.'

'—and Timmie was a bus girl at the department-store and Little Alphonse danced on the steps of the radio-station—'

'Well, if they was all local, what'd they want to move out West for?' Dot Sambrook asked.

'Reasons of finance,' the Prince said loftily.

'Hey—you know Holly in the Ultimates?'

'She is about to have a baby,' the Prince said.

'She was telling me—like Timmie and she and the other girl used to get out of school around noon; then they'd hitch over to St Botolph and just *beg* Galahad to let 'em record something. Then it'd get to bein' snack-time, so Mrs Trickett would fix pork and beans or bacon and beans and hamburgers—'

'And what's she to Galahad?' Dot Sambrook said. 'His auntie?'

'No-o,' the Prince demurred. 'She his big sister. A most charming lady. She take care of ever'thing here now.'

'*And* George,' Laverne giggled. 'The singing-dancing telephone-man.' She pinched her drinking-straw back in shape. 'But you four Princes—you was buddy-buddy with Galahad way back from the beginning, right?'

'When he signed us—we were the first. In his living-room. He said to us, "I can only promise you one thing. You're going to have hit-records."'

'Hey—and would you believe! I work for him and I ain't never even *seen* him!'

'He prefers to be secluded,' the Prince said reverently.

'So man, let him see-clude! Right? I ain't 'bout to mess with all o'them *guards* and—and 'lectric tangles, uh-*uh*!'

'I bumped into him once,' Dot Sambrook said. Her voice, as usual, betrayed no enthusiasm. 'When Kyle and me did *Tell Him Soon* for the Ultimates with Shirley. Before the session, this little bearded bloke comes up and says to me—like a bloody schoolmaster, right?— "That bit in the middle, that *whoo-hoo* bit, that's not Africa Records." He told us it didn't fit. We had to take it off the bloody song!'

'Too much,' Laverne laughed. 'And you had a hit.'

As the Prince rose, almost to the ceiling of the booth, she added, 'You all come by the hotel now after the show, hear? The Marrakesh.'

The Prince bowed. Clearly he had been deeply moved by the references to the president of Africa Records.

''F a thing didn't fit—he took it out,' the Prince declared. 'And when this whole town didn't fit, man, he got out of *it*. He,' the Prince said reverently, 'was an Undefeatist.'

The two husbands came through from the patio with their glasses. In Betty Tarlo's kitchen there was, between the Tarlos and their guests Lauren and Mooney Seli-mović, an instant of intense, cocktail-flushed, early evening happiness. How handsome they are, the wives thought, how good they smell. How beautiful they are, the men thought, how great the steak smells.

'Baby, please put music on,' Betty called.

'Music, o-oh-kay,' Dick Tarlo said. He was thirty, but with the earnestness of a man ten years younger. 'What do you want, Moon? I got Sinatra—Basie—Timmie Royale...'

It was Timmie they played, but cautiously, so that she would not be heard across the lawns of other homes on the Drive. All the suburbs stood still within their rancho-style fencing in the dusk, which was slightly perfumed by detergent.

'Oh Betty Tarlo, I'm all embarrassed! Hearts-of-lettuce salad. You shouldn't have, dear.'

There was wine, too, and candles outside, cupped in little goblets. Betty always made an occasion of dinner, though she saw Lauren every day. Their friendship was strengthened rather than otherwise by the uniformity of their hair and of the coloured shirts they wore, tied at the waist with gilt slave chains, and the twin Volvos both of them drove.

The steaks, broiled by Dick, were perfect. Afterwards they sat on the flickering patio and, in joy and comfort and delicious trepidation, passed around a marijuana cigarette. With her voice already a little slurred, Lauren said, 'Betty, tell me something, dear. How do you keep your eyes so nice and white?'

Betty looked at Dick. With his neat hair and truthful mouth, how handsome he was!

'Okay,' Mooney was saying, 'Okay, I'm ignorant, I know it. I admit that I know very little of the great institutions of this country—'

'The Guard is a state institution,' Dick corrected.

'Okay, Prof—of the state. I said I was ignorant.'

'—he sells automobiles very good,' Lauren put in.

Mooney appealed to Betty. 'What I'm saying *is*, I just never did manage to figure out what these guys *do* at the Armoury on a weekend.'

'I'll tell you that one,' Betty smiled, 'they have fun.'

'*We* have fun at the Lake,' remarked Lauren in some confusion.

'Sure is one heap of space you got out there, Richard.'

'Yeah, pretty big,' Dick said. 'The Guard can't use all of that. We rent one of the lots to the auto factory.'

'Like an old movie studio—say!' Mooney interjected. 'Know what they're showing on Channel Four at eleven-forty? *A Night at the Opera.*'

Lauren giggled with blue smoke up her nose.

'Oh, I know, everybody! A man flies round in a cloak, screaming. Did I get it right?'

'No-o.' The others laughed. 'That's *Phantom of the Opera.*'

'You know—that's why I feel really sorry for little kids,' Mooney said. 'Think of all the great flicks they're missing on the Late Show.'

Dick Tarlo drew deeply on the wicked cigarette.

'Sure—people say about the Guard "Oh, Kent State, you know". Killers. Trigger-happy. Those guys at Kent State lost their heads.'

'I think the National Guard has a very strong community motivation,' Betty added. 'But you never get publicity on that, do you, baby?'

Dick stared at her. How beautiful she was.

Lauren's eyes were now closed. In a soft passage of Timmie's voice, Lauren held her arms tight and murmured, 'Oh, I'd just give up anything to be able to sing that way.'

'They train us pretty tough,' Dick continued. 'Stipulated, two weekends in the month. Firearms practice —cold-weather school.'

'And one time,' Betty said, 'they all took a ride in a truck to Battle Creek Michigan and then came on right home.'

'—she just says—really—everything I want to say.'

'Huh?' Mooney stared at his wife.

'I'd give up anything to be able to sing like that,' Lauren told him sombrely.

'Oh hey now, wait a minute there!' Mooney protested, 'Me in the Guard! Hold on!'

'Mooney, you'd just love it. Wouldn't he, baby?'

'Me in the National Guard—ah Jees, come on.'

Abruptly, Lauren sat forward. 'I remembered, people!' she exclaimed. '*A Night at the Opera*, right?'

'Mooney, you'd just love it. Colonel Burlingame's the sweetest man—he's Dick's Colonel. Full of jokes and all kinds of fun, and they have real good community programmes at the Armoury, barbecues and, oh, dances and a big trailer and outboard show every Fall.'

'But,' Lauren said in a stage-whisper, 'aren't you *afraid*?' She put her fingertips to her mouth. 'Oh, excuse me.'

'I see it this way,' said Dick. 'Minimum career-interference. A spell with the Guard suits me a whole lot more than two years in a paddy-field when I was through with college.'

He looked at Betty, at the flicks of her hair above the mandarin collar, at her cheeks which burned slightly with the dying of the candles in their goblets.

'Not that I was trying to evade my responsibilities, you understand.' Nationalism surged in Dick Tarlo by way of the genitals. 'Shucks, I guess I owe Uncle Sam something.'

He felt her eyes on him.

'Way I see it is, I'm helping defend my home—my wife and country just as sure as those guys—'

The telephone rang inside the house. As Betty jumped up to get it, Mooney jokingly said, 'That'll be the riot.'

When the two men were left alone—for Lauren now floated on pillows without logic—Mooney resumed, 'So what does happen on those Guard weekends, Richard?'

Her head thrown back, through her tightened throat Lauren murmured, 'Just all the things I *ever* wanted to ... *she* can say. Give up anything to sing like...'

'Good to get away with the boys a spell?' Mooney inquired. A complicated reply filled Dick's head but the temptation to confide in another man was too strong. He chuckled.

'Boy, I'll tell you, Moon, that's some place for gags that Armoury. The Colonel's the worst one of all. No, really. Sure we kid around. Take Nat—you know Nat? Has a bad time home with his wife. Friday nights Nat gets in his pickup to go on training-weekend, and the guy's living!'

As Colonel Burlingame approached his exit on the Parkway, he made a wish. Now it had been granted. God had damned pot-roast. The Colonel was giving his first Press conference at Police Headquarters seated on a desk, holding one knee and rocking gently back and forth.

'We have conceded,' he replied, 'this would have been around ten-fifteen.'

'When that kid was beat-up by the Grailers?'

'No, we have conceded its origin to be a blind pig in the'—Colonel Burlingame gave the merest pause—the nigra section.'

Blind pigs are illegal black drinking establishments.

''M I hoggin' anyone's desk?' inquired the Colonel of the surrounding detectives.

'No that's okay, Gus, go ahead.'

'Was it Panthers, Colonel?'

Intensifying the wisdom of his manner, the Colonel replied, 'We-ell, bunch o' radicals at back of it somewheres, I guess.'

'Colonel,' said the black reporter, 'I am credibly informed that the club your units raided was not a blind pig. It was just a bar-room with music.'

174

The Colonel scratched his head.

'Now look-ee,' he answered in a homespun way, 'that ol' place wasn't legal. Now, just 'cause there's a few guys in there screamin' hippy songs—doesn't mean it's a supper-club.' He crinkled his eyes at the corner. 'Right?'

'Colonel Burlingame—'

'Shucks, call me Gus. Ever'body does.'

'Is it correct that many of your men on the—'

'Could you talk up, son?'

'Is it correct that many of your men on the street are college-kids?'

' "College-kids",' the Colonel mused upon the phrase. 'Now we got college-*graduates*. Right about now that's the only sort we take into the Guard. I could walk you out on that street tonight and introduce you to a Doctor of Political Science of the State University,' the Colonel said with sudden pride.

'But we have veterans; Legion of Honour guys. They'll handle anything you toss 'em.'

He did not add that most of these splendid personalities were absent at half-yearly camp in Michigan.

'How many casualties have you sustained to this point, Colonel?' the black reporter asked.

'National Guard units,' the Colonel intoned, rocking back and forward, 'do not assume, in time of civil emergency, the functions of the Police Department. Our purpose is to lend support to the regular peace-keeping agencies in Tall-Man squads of—

'—We-ell,' the Colonel admitted, 'we lost one feller.'

'Where was that, Gus?'

'At a road-block.'

The Colonel did not feel it necessary to add that the Guardsman had been shot by another Guardsman, aged eighteen, firing from the opposite side of the junction in an attempt to wound a car which had disregarded their screams of 'Halt'.

175

'Guess we never did find out where that one came from,' said the Colonel.

'Your units are on the streets with M4s?'

'Check.'

'Gas?'

'Now hold on a minute,' the Colonel said gently. 'This isn't a Detroit or Newark, New Jersey situation. This is a few kids burning up some parade buggies in Rovira Circle. So we just have to bring out a little muscle down there.'

He showed them a map of the downtown area in which the good men, his patrolling units, were indicated by stars. Positioned at intervals around the fountains in Rovira Circle, they would presently move down Estrella Avenue and outwards to bring reason and light into darker thoroughfares.

'So your anticipations are against the committal of heavy-armament, right, Gus?'

'Tanks,' the black reporter elucidated.

The Colonel appeared shocked.

'We anticipate no such order. Gosh darn-it!' His eyes crinkled up. *'Tanks!'*

The Press Conference broke up. The black reporter left but the rest stayed on, chatting.

'Now I'll tell you boys'—The Colonel said, 'we may have started out kinda raggity, it being on a weekend and all. But you cain't hardly call it a riot as of now. You boys could all go on home to supper.

'You asked about morale there. Listen, I'm having to keep people back at the Armoury. I have to tell these guys, "Sergeant—*someone* has to stay behind and answer the phone."'

But there was a hitch in the confident arrangements of Colonel Burlingame. A flourish unforeseen by the individuals with neat beards who, at home in Detroit, calculated the riot would have died now, like the lights in a pinball-machine.

It was the weather. It happened sometimes—not every year. After the weak, exhausting day, a beautiful evening. The softest breeze moving a shrub at a blood-red wall. The sudden lightening of the spirit which accompanies full inflation of the lungs. Having ventured to their front-stoops and open windows, people went farther, to the very limit of living. They walked. And, like all who seldom walk, they discovered wonder in it.

All the lower avenues of the city went strolling; full of tolerance represented by bicycles. In the walking of black people, unlike white, there is the important factor of direction. Something had been happening in Rovira Circle and thus that stroll led finally down Estrella Avenue to see what it was. In the Africa Records building, George came upstairs with his long handled dustpan and thought there must be a second parade.

In a way, so it was. This late on a Saturday night, the boulevard belonged to them. Ahead, the honeycomb of skyscraper lights, freed of the hag shapes that held them, took on a winking and magnetic beauty. It was as if all of them suddenly felt they were walking in the city that the sound of Africa Records suggested: the city of furs and chord-sharp cloth, where every man swung along with brand-new cuffs and every girl's voice was Timmie Royale's.

And so thousands surged up towards the pink fountains in Rovira Circle; loosely but with an internal tumult that found pleasure in everything—the bums asleep in the doorways, the caged liquor-stores, the progress of a roadsweeper bouncing on its brushes. More joined in and more, wearing long shorts and sunburst shirts and formal shirts and no shirts, pink and albino wigs and leopard coats, carrying babies in slings, tactfully drinking from clenched paper bags, selling copies of *Muhammad Speaks*, and balloons and brooches and dresses on hangers, but above all, laughing. Above all, unlike the Grailer parade, belonging to that place and fulfilling thereby, the fundamental human obligation. With the Africa sounds thrumming in their heads and bodies, the crowd like the music was in good taste.

But for the National Guard units in Rovira Circle life was not, as it had become for Colonel Burlingame, an adventure playground. They were unhappy—or rather, perplexed in the worst of ways. They did not know how to put one foot in front of the other.

The Army Manual, which also governs the actions of the National Guard, is unequivocal on this point.

They must proceed with painful stealth.

Their eyes must, in agony, canvass back-lots and alleys for sniper-fire; for flying rocks and garage-wrenches and builder's bricks with firecrackers lodged inside.

Their eyes must constantly watch above them—therefore tonight the Guardsmen kept bumping into people, and sometimes, being Doctors of Philosophy or of Political Science, they murmured 'Excuse me'.

Men alone in the dark forests of anarchy, they discovered themselves surrounded, twirled and engulfed by an enormous, gleaming, jollificating crowd.

It was, above all, hideously embarrassing.

'He-ey!'

'Hey, sojer!'

'Hey, Action Man, walk for me, baby!'

'Sir, do you rock and roll?'

'Hey brother, don't light up when yo' gets in church!'

'Oh, ain't they *cute*! They is *cute*!'

Now they saw it—a car tipped in blazing fish-bones: a suite of furniture being lifted carefully through a broken store window.

Now they didn't.

Even the bottles popping on the ground next to their boots seemed as impalpable as sighs.

Out of the front of a supermarket, a boy came on the mime of his baseball shoes, carrying a six-pack of soft drinks. Nearby, a group of Guardsmen stood in anxious conference.

The Army Manual distinctly states—

There was a crack like the slamming of a window.

In time of civil emergency, looters are shot.

The boy lay on the sidewalk crying noiselessly, hidden by their olive-green legs.

The six-pack he still held close to the T-shirt he had put on that morning as a child of eleven.

It was diet-cola.

He didn't even like it.

The Guardsman who had fired, turned towards the crowd.

Chinstraps loose, eyes hidden under his helmet.

His M4 could penetrate four consecutive human bodies.

Perfect murderer of babies.

'—*Listen!*' he sobbed.

He was Specialist 4 Richard S. Tarlo and right now he wanted to be at home with his young wife in the suburbs watching *A Night at the Opera* on The Late Show.

'*Listen!*

'—as far as I'm concerned, anybody that threatens my personal safety is my personal—

'Only a kid. Sure he is. But in the dark he—throws a bottle from the tenth storey, you're sitting there with no cover on your jeep—

'Oh my God! We let it go too far!'

The boy was lifted up. His face showed in the circular light that ducked on the ambulance-roof.

179

'Same as with a puppy,' Tarlo wept. 'If he messes up the carpet and you let it go, he does it again.

'He won't do it again if you beat his brains out.'

There was one accurate view only; as was proper, from the WAAB News helicopter. Turning from the blue-beaded pipe of light that was Estrella Avenue, it dipped for a moment in the night to see the city spread like a tuxedo-coat, lovingly brocaded with flame.

As the WAAB reporter called his station, he found the channel interrupted by a short-wave conversation from the ground: a voice, thickened by static and terror gabbling: '—the Marrakesh Hotel is a known house of prostitution.'

'Huh?' said the helicopter pilot.

'—getting some sorta snarlup here.'

As they listened, a second, very calm voice interrupted:

'Nat, do you still read me?'

'I read you, Colonel.'

'Come on, Nat, you (crackle)—call me Gus.'

'Must be a Police frequency,' said the WAAB reporter.

'—(crackle)—exact position, Nat?'

'Guarding the Lake Superior Life Insurance Building.'

'—that's at Estrella and—'

'Estrella and Lamont. Lake Superior are a black outfit but they won't insure Panthers or Black Nationalists or any of that stuff, Colonel—Gus.'

'Yeah, Nat. You sure there's firing across the street?'

'The Marrakesh is a known house of prostitution—(crackle)—take prostitutes outa there...' The voices ceased.

'That's the Guard,' remarked the helicopter pilot.

The voices were picked up again a few minutes later. The helicopter had paused over the ugly districts of dark crimson where the boulevard had died, fractured into a million tepid skylights.

'I think we got something,' said the WAAB reporter.

'—*Colonel!*'

'Nat—the prowlcar's there on Lamont. Over.'

'—Colonel! *Gus!*'

'You got all the police support you need—over.' The calm voice reassured. The other ran away in a monotony of terror. The calm voice said, 'Can you speak up any, Nat? Over.'

'—of the cops came out on the hotel parking-lot and tells me there's three hippies inside that got it. I goes inside to check it out. One's dead in the lobby—the room-clerk. There's another one still kickin' ...'

'Ho-old on there now. Are those black kids, Nat? Over.'

'One white woman. From Eng-land. There's a whole bunch of 'em in town tonight screamin' hippy songs.' Recovering a little, the voice took on a desperate note of corncob humour:

'Wheeee, and I thought maybe I'd get me a night's sleep tonight.'

'That guy,' the helicopter-pilot remarked, 'has trouble with his wife.'

Abandoning rusticity, the voice moaned:

'Jeezus, Colonel, those *cops!*'

The voices fell away and rose again in the whipping of the helicopter.

'—a big black kid; musta stood seven feet tall and weighed ... I dunno, two-eighty or ninety. He's got a high-hat, you know? With ribbons.'

'Yeah, Nat. You're lookin' good.'

The other voice replied with a strangled sound.

'I guess the kid in the high-hat musta got fresh. I guess the cops belted him, Colonel.'

'Yeah, Nat, yeah—over.'

'—cops are takin' those kids outside, pretending to shoot over their heads. Colonel—I just see this cop go out with this little nigra girl with one heap 'o hair. Her hair way up to here. The shotgun went off. I knew he'd shot her: Jeezus, Colonel, what do I *do*? I just came out for laughs. Just a few laughs. It's good to cook out with all the guys. My God, what do I *do*? I'm gonna get all kinds of lawsuits against me ...'

'Now ho-old on there, Nat...'

'I told 'em,' the voice babbled.

—Friday nights, when he went on Guard training, was when he started to live.

'I told 'em, "I'm having nothin' to do with all this, I'm gonna go guard the Lake Superior Insurance Building" and right then these cops are taking the English girl out, pretending to shoot over her head and—'

'Nat—do you still read me, Nat? Over.'

'Jeezus, Colonel, what am I goin' to *do*? I gotta get my number took outa the book...'

In the progress of a tank, there is something spell-binding, as in that of a clumsy person among teacups.

Colonel Burlingame had kept his word. The million tiny squeaks and swivels, the racy turret, the elegant gun and creamy new star which settled all to rest on South Estrella, just short of the Africa Records build-ing, belonged, not to a tank but to a self-propelled .155 gun that squeaked partly for being brand-new: lovely, it smelled of the paint of new toys, begged to be picked up and turned in the hand, and behind it, the pink fountains in Rovira Circle played like a foaming Christmas window.

When the .155 was comfortable, a file of Guardsmen wearing gas-masks which gave them the faces of grass-hoppers, appeared from either side of it and spread a line across the boulevard. Their M4s they flourished slightly aloft in one hand, as cavalrymen with Carbines. Behind them, six more appeared. These moved with greater—indeed, with almost excessive—modesty, as befits the elite of society in war or peace. They were trained marksmen. Their weapons swaggered with telescopes. The movement was impeccable, with no trace in it of self-conciousness. When it was complete, from their masks the line spoke a single word:

'*Airborne!*'

They were not under Colonel Burlingame's command —would, indeed, have been outraged at association with it. Nor were the Doctors of Political Science nor breakfast-food salesmen for whom the social-life only began on Friday nights, in the grease and green canvas and mashed-potato scents of the Armoury. They were, instead, heroes. They belonged to 186th Special Forces (Airborne), a crack reserve of parachute militia to whom, above all, singularity of movement was vital and beautiful. Their war-cry they would utter even on quite ordinary occasions, such as lining up in mess-hall.

The people, whose way they superfluously barred, greeted them warmly.

'Uh, what's that you say, brother?'

'*Airborne!*' the line repeated.

Out of the crowd flickering with enjoyment and the reflection of fire, a car drove up and stopped before the .155, right under the elegant spill of the gun. The shirt-front and the smile glinted of the man who got out. He walked along the line, giving out chocolate and chewing-gum.

'*Airborne!*'

'Oh—Airborne,' the crowd delightedly echoed; and from Airborne's groin up to its trigger-finger, the vivid, white annoyance rose and curled.

Chocolate! Chewing-gum!

Airborne had been summoned and had obeyed. They

had left their volleyball, their canoe-building, their Eagle Scout troops. No sacrifice, would it hinder despoliation of the Constitution and their little daughters by laughing black men, was too much.

Airborne were arisen, but not merely at the direction of the Army Manual. Theirs were the most glittering traditions of the United States Militia. They performed at pageants. Shoulder-to-shoulder they stood beside every hero of recruitment literature—the Georgetown Rifles who drove the British from the field with only tomahawks, and the Richmond Blues, the old 'Silk Stockings' of New York City, the sacred Irregulars of George Washington himself.

They were the stars at the finish of the picture.

Chocolate? Chewing gum?

Their enemy they knew. Weekends of film-slide and lecture had taught them: their enemy wore Zulu beards and dark glasses, or else assumed the shape of an army of hippies, in regiments and squadrons, with mystical powers of infiltration, who swore an oath that every day they would seek some fresh way of insulting The Flag; who wore coloured blankets in the concealment of which they aborted babies, evaded their military obligation or smoked—as the instructing Major had pronounced it 'C'narbis'. The enemy were the hordes of darkness and the liberal point of view and Airborne, the men who faced them.

But what did they find? Nothing but a few kids looting stores. A few burnt-out carnival buggies in the Circle. Armoury kids trying to handle it, so scared that Airborne's own Colonel had to order a bunch of them to unload their weapons.

No armies of the dark; only an audience.

Laughing and staring.

And chocolate! Chewing-gum!

Beside the .155, a lieutenant spoke into his electric

megaphone. Obligingly, the crowd withdrew a few yards, leaving behind the madman who had distributed the candy. He remained leaning against the fins of his car, gazing up at the gun. His white shirt glinted, and his teeth as he smiled at the passion of the lieutenant: then, reaching into the front seat of the car, he pulled out—

A gun.

At last.

Ten on one knee together. Greedy, bolted song of safety catches. Choose a face, laughing and black.

I know what you'd like to do to my wife

I see you teasing me with your swaying black ass

You deserve to die, Red Man

He pulled out—his *hat*!

One shot only was loosed, and crisply rang about the façade of the Africa Records building. Somehow, possibly by his scream, the lieutenant restrained Airborne from firing a volley of twenty. But they might have done just as well, since bullets blood-whipping through four bodies at once are more easily called back than certain sounds, the music of bolts drawn all together.

On Estrella Avenue, outside the Africa Records building, an order of things seemed to correct itself in that moment. There was a pause, as if for final breath; then, from one side all irritation had passed and from the other, all jollity. Obedient at last to Colonel Burlingame's diagram, two armies faced one another. One of them, good. One, bad. Each crackling with the wickedness of the other.

The armies moved together, almost in slow motion in the firelight. She screamed and ran up between them.

Some lovely girl might still the heart of a self-propelled gun, but not Pearl Aiken. She was black—black is very often plain. She showed her legs only because her friends did. As she screamed, it sounded like her mother, if that was the only voice Pearl had.

Her voice was Timmie's. What Pearl felt was Timmie Royale on the long, high note of love for someone handsome and arms stretched up to feel the finish of the stars. White women too, such as Lauren Selimović in her prison of kitchen-pine, had discovered their hearts might speak through Timmie, but it was not the spring of the white women's dreams that was menaced.

Pearl's arms were only short. With her cheek against its cold corner, she tried, nevertheless, to encircle the Africa Records building with them, to protect and keep for ever the dresses and the sounds which, for Pearl, were still inside.

George was there somewhere, sleeping.

But no stars now.